A LITERARY SCANDAL

LIBBY HOWARD

Created with Vellum

CHAPTER 1

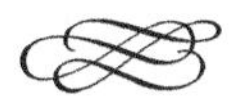

"I've been dying to show you something," I told Kat as I handed her a glass of wine. Our neighborhood porch happy hour had expanded, and there were evenings when it felt like half the town was milling about on my porch, drinking wine and shedding the weight of the work day. Kat was here early, even before Daisy had arrived, and she looked like she seriously needed that glass of Chardonnay.

"Your latest knitting project?" She sipped the wine and watched me dig into the Vera Bradley tote I was using as a craft bag.

"Yeah." I handed her the scarf, transported back in time to when I was standing beside my fifth-grade science project, waiting for the judges to comment.

"This is beautiful, Kay." She handed it back to me. "I love that yarn, and the pattern is really pretty."

My heart sank. "But?"

"It's beautiful," she insisted. "Wear it. Enjoy it. Be happy that you've got something beautiful on that you made with your own hands. And when you're ready to start your next project, ask me to come over and I'll walk you through the stitches."

"Because I didn't get these stitches right?" I looked down at the scarf.

Kat leaned over me. "See this decrease here? You're doing both decreases on either side of the central pattern as knit-two-together. You need to do a slip-knit-passover on this one so the knitted stitch is angling in the right direction. They should look like they're hugging the pattern, drawing the eye toward the eyelet stitches."

"Oh." I'd worked so hard on it too.

"Kay, no one will see the difference. Wear it. It's beautiful, and you made it yourself. Be proud of that."

"But it's not perfect." I contemplated pounding down my wine, maybe pounding down the entire bottle. "I wanted it to be perfect."

"Which is why I pointed it out to you. Otherwise I would have kept my mouth shut. This is how you learn. I can't tell you how many sweaters I have with tiny little flaws in the pattern where I miscounted, or forgot a yarn-over, or dropped a stitch and wove it back in wrong. I wear every one of them with pride. They're gorgeous and no one but me knows there's a tiny little human mistake in them. Doesn't matter. I love them anyway."

I squinted down at the scarf, looking at the decreases slanted the wrong way. "So, slip-knit-passover, huh?"

"Call me and I'll show you. I'll even show you how to do a Fair Isle stitch holding the background color yarn in your left hand. You'll be making sweaters and knitting lace in no time."

I laughed. "Think I'm going to stick with simple scarves for a while. They're going to be my Secret Santa gifts this year."

"Ooh, I know who I want getting my name this year,

then." Daisy clomped up the stairs to my porch, eyeing the scarf. "That's pretty. I want one in blue."

She was getting one in blue; she just didn't know it yet. I poured Daisy a glass of wine then fired up a second one as I saw Suzette walking down the sidewalk.

"So...Luanne Trainor." Daisy's eyebrows wiggled as she took the glass of wine.

"I know. It was quite the surprise, a last-minute addition to the theater's speaker series," I said. My friend Nancy was all a-flurry getting things organized just-so for the big event. We didn't often get big-names in Locust Point or Milford, and according to Nancy, Luanne Trainor was A-list big.

"Do you have tickets?" Kat gave a quick hop, clutching her wine glass in both hands. "I can't wait. I've read every one of her novels. Rumor has it there's a film in the works."

"Oh, I'll be there, meet-and-greet and all." Daisy shot me a grin. "I've got connections, you know."

Kat turned to me, her eyebrows raised.

"I'm in charge of hospitality," I confessed. "Nancy Fishman roped me into it, probably because she wanted me to make my icebox cake for the reception after the lecture."

Daisy rolled her eyes. "It's not a lecture, Professor Carrera, it's a presentation and a book signing. And the reason Nancy Fishman asked you to host it is because you're the only woman in town who hasn't read Luanne Trainor's novels. Thus, you're the only woman in town that isn't likely to go all fangirl on her and drool on her fancy designer shoes or chain her to a bed and threaten to break her legs if she didn't have Roman wind up with Trelanie."

Oh, good grief. "No, I'm sure it's the icebox cake."

"You gals talking about Luanne Trainor?" Suzette huffed, hopping up the final step and reaching toward me for the outstretched glass of Chardonnay. "I just read the first in her

Infernal Awakenings series. Wow. Needed a cold shower after that one."

Maybe I needed to pick up these books. Although, given that I was a recent widow, anything that made me run for a cold shower probably wasn't something I wanted on my reading list.

"Her Fanged Darkness series is even hotter," Kat confessed. "Will was ready to barricade himself in the man cave by the time I'd finished book six. He swore if I read anything else by that woman, he was going to need to ask his doctor for Viagra."

Daisy laughed. "Right. The man protests too much, methinks. Are you gals rooting for Roman and Trelanie? Or do you think he's going to go all dark-side and ditch her for that 'ho Morgana?"

"Daisy!" I scolded, shocked that my friend who was all about empowering women and smashing the patriarchal establishments would even refer to a fictional character as a 'ho.

"Do you think there's really going to be a film?" Suzette asked. "How the heck are they going to rate that movie? I mean, is there a Z rating or something? A quintuple X?"

"Oh, the books aren't that explicit.... are they?" I frowned and picked up my wine, once more contemplating downing the contents. When Nancy had first approached me about running hospitality for this last-minute guest of Milford Theater's speaker series, I'd assumed I'd be making nice to an award-winning journalist, or someone who wrote literary fiction, like The Secret Life of Bees or something. Not smutty novels featuring vampires and demons as the hot love interests.

Okay, maybe I was being overly snobby here. I'd certainly enjoyed my share of bodice rippers and dime-store romances over the years. Why *shouldn't* the author of an insanely popular New York Times bestselling series deliver a presentation and graciously mingle with fans at a book signing? It's not like she was going to be acting out scenes from her novels or anything.

I snickered at the idea, thinking that I probably should read a few of these woman's books before I hauled down to pick her up at the airport and proceeded to spend two days in her company, ensuring her comfort and happiness and guaranteeing that the meet-and-greet signing post lecture, or presentation, went smoothly. I had a bunch of them upstairs on my nightstand, given to me by a very adamant Daisy who insisted I take her well-worn, dog-eared paperbacks.

"Are y'all talking Luanne Trainor here?" Olive climbed my steps, fanning her face with a dramatic hand. "Woo. That's some steamy stuff there, girls."

The woman tossed her hair over her shoulder, beads clacking, and gave me a wink as she reached for a glass. Olive had become a regular at our porch-parties the last month and was practically like a neighbor at this point.

"I got our tickets," Suzette told her. "Third row. I sprang for the meet-and-greet as well."

Olive poured her wine then grinned over at the other woman. "Thanks. I'll pick up dinner in return. Greek? That Ethiopian place in Stallworth? Or do you want to try the new gastro pub in downtown Milford?"

"Ethiopian?" Suzette's eyes sparkled.

"You'll love it," I told her. "The food comes in little separate piles on these huge metal trays and you scoop it up by hand with spongy buckwheat pancakes and eat it like a makeshift soft taco. Get the lamb, or the goat if they have it."

Eli and I used to eat there. My mind drifted back to memories of us sharing a dinner in the dimly lit basement restaurant, walking among the galleries and antique shops afterward, then swinging in for a quick gelato before heading home. I'd hold his hand, practically dozing as our car hummed over the back roads from Stallworth to Locust Point, lulled into a somnolent state by the food and the languid romance of the evening.

"When are you picking her up from the airport?" Daisy asked me, interrupting my trip down memory lane. "Can I hide in your trunk and be a creepy stalker woman?"

"Tomorrow morning, and no." I laughed. J.T. had given me Friday off, trading my lost salary for free advertising at the event. I'm not sure what he thought a few hundred rabid Luanne Trainor readers were going to want with an investigations and bail bonds firm, though. Maybe for all the divorces when the ladies left their husbands for sexy, brooding vampires? Or for all the DWIs after the meet-and-greet, although hopefully the volunteer bartenders would be savvy enough to prevent that sort of thing.

"So, what does being a host entail?" Kat asked. "Chauffeur? Food pick-up and delivery? Making sure there are no green M&Ms in the bowl in the dressing room?"

I grimaced. "All of the above. Nancy is taking care of the room set-up, the food and beverages, and the volunteer servers, but I need to make sure the signing process goes smoothly, and pretty much run around like a chicken with my head cut off, doing whatever Ms. Trainor wants me to do."

"You get to basically have two days of one-on-one with her." Suzette's voice was wistful with a touch of envy. "I wonder what she's really like? I've read some interviews with her and saw a video of her presentation at some conference, but that's not really a good indication of what someone's like, you know?"

I did know. Almost thirty years in journalism and I'd done plenty of interviews where my subjects were practiced and careful about the words they spoke as well as the image they projected.

"I promise I'll give you all the details," I told her. "Everything from when she has spinach between her teeth to her weird taste in music."

"I just want to know if Trelanie and Roman end up together," Kat told me. "He needs her. She is the only one who can heal his tortured vampire soul."

"How about him healing *her* soul?" I teased. "Or, at the very least, taking out the garbage every Wednesday night and remembering to pick up milk on the way home from work. That's the stuff that true love is built on."

"It's not about garbage night and milk," Daisy informed me. "It's about his smooth moves in the bedroom. Boom-chicka-wow-wow."

I swatted Daisy's arm and laughed but I was thinking about Eli and his accident and how long it had been since there had been any boom-chicka-wow-wow for me. No, love *was* about the garbage night and the milk. Actually, it was about the companionship, the weaving together of two lives, the building of something so strong it withstood the test of time, the test of catastrophic medical issues...and the forever loss of boom-chicka-wow-wow.

"Hush, the menfolk are coming." Kat grinned and waved a hand toward where her husband was heading up the sidewalk and Judge Beck was pulling in the driveway.

Sometimes Kat's husband Will would join us, as would Bert Peter from across the street, and Bob Simmons from down the block. The men always held their glasses of wine like we were serving them strychnine, and stood around with that deer-in-headlights expression, eventually huddling together at the end of the porch to discuss lawn mowing techniques or what the greens looked like on the city golf course while we talked, laughed, and shrieked like harpies.

We wouldn't see the menfolk for a week or two, then they'd come back, inexorably drawn by our odd womanly ritual, trying to discern the mysteries of the female sex by observing our weekly, after-work bonding.

Judge Beck knew better. He'd exchange a few polite words, then flee inside to wait for our happy hour to be over. I took pity on him and tried to have the more gender-neutral neighborhood barbeque parties once a month throughout the summer.

Will paused and waited for the judge to exit his car. They spoke, then headed up the stairs side-by-side. This time, as Will poured himself some wine, Judge Beck picked up a glass and held it out for the other man to fill.

I nearly fell over in shock. "Are you joining us tonight?" I asked him. "I mean, you're always welcome, you know."

"Just the one glass." He held it up in a toast, clinking it against mine. "I've got some work I need to do, but I thought I'd join you for a quick drink."

Heather had the kids on a two-week vacation, and Judge Beck had been drowning himself in work. It had become his habit to put in long hours when he didn't have the kids so he could shorten his workload for the weeks he did have them, but this was different. Two weeks they'd be gone. I missed them too, but for the judge, it was as if they'd been gone forever. From a few things he'd let slip, I knew his and Heather's divorce proceedings had hit a rough patch. That was probably as much the reason for his insane workload lately as missing his children.

I did my best to make sure he had a decent dinner to warm up whenever he got home, and some coffee and homemade pastries ready and waiting for when he woke up and dashed out the door to work, but other than that, I tried to let him deal with things in his own way. I was walking a fine line between being a supportive friend and prying. And it was hard because I missed him just as much as I missed the kids. He'd hardly been home at all in the last week, and when he was he'd been in the dining room, nose-deep in papers. It was a shock seeing him pull in the driveway before eight o'clock. And a double shock seeing him mingling with the neighbors on the porch, a glass of wine in his hand.

"You work too hard," I told him, deciding the supportive friend me needed to nudge him out of his workaholic mood a bit. "We should do a movie night."

He smiled, lines crinkling up at the edges of his hazel eyes. "That sounds fun, but don't you have some high-society event thing you're doing this weekend?"

"Luanne Trainor," I told him. "She's more high-profile than high-society. Maybe tomorrow night if she doesn't have me running errands. Or Sunday once I drop her off at the airport."

"I'll pencil it in." He took a sip of wine then looked around at the crowd on our porch. "You're becoming quite the socialite, Kay. Between these happy hours and the barbeques, you've got something going on most days of the week."

I eyed him in concern. "Is it too much? It's just been such a nice summer. If it's too much—"

"I meant it as a compliment, Kay. You probably weren't able to entertain much at all the last ten years, and from what you've told me, you and Eli were very social before his accident. I think it's wonderful that you're having the neighbors over and making new friends."

"Does it disrupt your work?" I was so worried that he'd been staying late at the office because my happy hours were something he didn't want to face. It wasn't like he'd ever joined us before today. Maybe I needed to stop them. Maybe we could move them over to Kat's house instead. Or Daisy's.

"No, it does not. I like it. And once my work settles down

a bit, I intend to join you more often. Especially now that I know it's not just a women-only thing."

"Silly, you're always welcome. Will and some of the other men have been coming off and on for the last few months."

He raised an eyebrow. "Off and on being the key phrase. They always look terrified, huddled over in the corner with their wine. I figured I was being the smart one, beating a hasty retreat into the house."

"Well, they've clearly gotten over their fear of us ladies." I gestured over to where Will was laughing over something with Suzette and Daisy. "Time for you to come out of hiding and join us."

"I will." He drained the wine glass and set it down on the table. "But tonight…"

"Tonight is work." I gave him a sympathetic smile. "There's chicken and mushroom sauce in the Crock-Pot, and rice in the warmer. Help yourself."

His smile was warm. "I'd starve if it wasn't for you, Kay. You know that, right?"

"Yes, I know that. Now get in there and get your work done. I've got big plans for us this weekend and I don't want some embezzlement case honing in on our movie time."

He saluted then grabbed his briefcase and headed for the door, passing right through the shadow that was forming just off to my left. I scowled, because this shadow wasn't the one I'd come to affectionately think of as Eli, the one that sat beside me while I watched television or read, the one that hovered comfortingly in my bedroom at night and watched over me as I gardened. No, this ghost was one I thought I'd gotten rid of when I'd taken Peony Smith down to the police station to confess her crimes. This ghost was Holt Dupree.

CHAPTER 2

"Knock over the wine and you're finished," I hissed at the shadow.

I didn't usually try to communicate with the spirits I saw in my peripheral vision, but Holt was proving to be a pain in the butt. From the first time he'd shown up in my kitchen after his death, he'd been knocking potatoes off my counter, pushing silverware off tables, and even overturning Taco's food bowl.

That last one he'd only done once. My cat normally avoided the ghosts, but no one messed with his food and lived to tell the tale. There had been a lot of hissing, upraised fur, and swatting at the shadow that night. Afterward, I noticed Holt's ghost gave my cat a wide berth.

I only wished he'd do the same to me—as in go haunt some other house and some other person. Poltergeist aside, I didn't want him around. Eli's spirit was a comforting presence. Holt's constantly reminded me of how a young life could be cut short, and about the girl who was waiting in juvenile court while her lawyer struggled to cut a plea deal. I felt sorry for her. I felt sorry for Holt. And watching a glass wobble on the table, I felt sorry for me.

"Oh, no you don't." The glass toppled on its side and I caught it before it rolled off the table. "Leave the breakables alone, if you please, or I'll be forced to bring Taco out of the house and sic him on you."

I shot a sideways glare at the ghost and moved over to where Daisy and Will were arguing over the chances of the local high school varsity football team making it to state this year. Hopefully Holt would follow me. Hopefully he'd dig the conversation about his favorite sport and follow Will home.

The dancing fairy statue at the bottom of my stairs teetered, then fell into the dirt. Seconds later, my mailbox door opened then shut with a snap. I squeezed my eyes shut and counted to ten, but when I opened them, I saw Holt's spirit kicking pebbles against the tires of Judge Beck's SUV.

I left Daisy and Will to their discussion and sidled up to Olive. "Can I ask your professional opinion on something?"

She grinned. "Accounting? Or the other profession?"

Olive was a friend of Daisy's, an accounting director at a local land developer, and a medium. She'd helped me contact Mabel Stevens' ghost back when the woman had been haunting my antique sideboard. Our interactions since then had been only social, but once again, I needed her help.

"You know I see ghosts, right? Not just the one who'd attached herself to my sideboard, but other ones. Murder victims. They tend to go away once their body is discovered or someone is arrested for killing them. Well, most of them anyway."

She nodded. "But you have a few who are sticking around? Not all spirits remain among the living for closure. Some have other motivations."

I grimaced. "I don't mind Mr. Peter across the street. He keeps to himself and I really don't see him all that often.

When I do, he's usually puttering around in the yard or hanging out on his front porch."

"He's attached to his home, it seems." Olive took a sip of her wine. "Those sorts of ghosts are here for the long haul. They do eventually move on, but it could be after hundreds of years."

My jaw dropped open. "Hundreds? I mean, I'm sure there are ghosts from Civil War battles still around, but do many stay for *hundreds of years*?"

She nodded. "Not so many around here, but in Europe there are some ghosts that have stuck it out for seven, eight hundred years. It depends on what they've attached themselves to and the circumstances of their death. Ones that haunt a house or castle can still be milling about even when it's in ruins. Usually if the building is completely demolished, they leave, though. Others that died on a battlefield can be there for a very long time. They're attached to the spot they died. Those are usually the ones who had a traumatic death. The house-haunting ones usually tend to be protecting their home, or just unwilling to leave their lives."

"I don't know why this one attached itself to me," I grumbled. "He's driving me crazy."

"Which one?" Olive patted me on the shoulder. "You've got two spirits here, you know."

The one I'd come to think of as Eli could stay. Holt needed to go.

"The young one," I told her. "He's knocking stuff over and making a pest of himself. I'm positive it's Holt Dupree's ghost, and I don't understand why he's bothering me like this. I didn't know him personally, and someone's already confessed to his murder and is in juvie."

Peony. Yes, she was a minor. No, nobody was supposed to know the name of a minor being charged with a crime, but Locust Point was a small town and gossip spread like wildfire. Everyone knew exactly who was responsible for our local celebrity's death.

"Maybe there's other folks that contributed to his death that need to be brought to light?"

I shook my head. "They arrested Buck Stanford for the car tampering. Does Holt need everyone who double-parked in his space to pay for their crimes before he leaves or something? Because that's not really my responsibility, you know."

She chuckled. "That, or he's staying around because he just doesn't want to leave."

"But why me?" I pressed. "Why not haunt the spot in the road where he went into the ditch? Or his mother's house? Or Violet Smith?"

Not that I really wanted poor Violet to have a poltergeist hanging around, but it would make more sense for Holt to be attached to the love of his life rather than some sixty-year-old, widowed, skip tracer who he'd probably only met once in passing.

"Maybe he thinks you're interesting." Olive shrugged. "You did find out all the details of his murder, including that his car was tampered with. You did get that girl to confess."

"So he's now a ghostly amateur sleuth?" I took a gulp of my wine, not pleased at the idea of his shadowy form dogging my heels as I went about my work. "Is there any way I can get rid of him, Olive? Can I bury garlic around the perimeter of my house or something?"

She laughed. "He's not a vampire."

"Seriously. Is there some way to convince him to head toward the light? Or at the very least, head toward some other section of town—preferably one I don't frequent?"

"I can't force a spirit to leave this plane of existence and I'm not the right sort of medium to ward against ghosts. You'd need someone who could smudge your house or make you an amulet of protection. Something like that."

I wrinkled my nose, not really liking those ideas. Daisy did the smudging thing, but I think that was more to align the energies or something. Plus, I didn't want *Eli's* ghost to leave, just Holt's, so that ruled out the smudge-against-ghosts idea. And an amulet…that was a bit too woo-woo for me.

"I can talk to him for you," Olive offered. "Most people I deal with want to connect with the spirits of their lost loved ones, but I occasionally help someone with a poltergeist case. Sometimes a ghost can be reasoned with."

"And convinced to leave?" I asked hopefully.

She grinned. "Or at least convinced to confine their activities to the shed out back, or to leave the breakables alone. Sometimes you can make a deal. Lots of times the ghosts just want to have their story heard or be recognized as present."

I thought about Mabel, and how she'd wanted her story known. She'd stayed around to make sure *someone* found that letter and knew what happened to her lover and her sister, that someone knew the horrible bargain she'd made to keep her daughter safe.

"Thanks, Olive. Anything you could do would be very much appreciated."

She clinked her wine glass with mine. "Tomorrow night then?"

I had to pick up Luanne Trainor from the airport and get her settled in to the little bed and breakfast in downtown Milford where she was staying, but after that I wouldn't have anything else on my schedule until the following day.

Oh, no. Judge Beck and the movie. I'd feel terrible canceling on him when I'd just got him to agree to set the work aside for one night. But Olive was doing me a favor here, and I really had to work around her schedule. The judge and I would have to push our movie night back to Sunday. Or maybe if we made it late on Friday, after Olive had left, we could have popcorn and bean dip and little sausage rolls. Sort of a late-night party.

"Friday night is perfect," I told Olive. "Nine o'clock?" Olive preferred to connect with the spirit world after dark, although she said she sometimes could communicate during daylight hours if a ghost was particularly motivated and cooperative.

"Let's make it ten, just to make sure the sun is down all the way." She wrinkled her nose.

"It's a date." Now I just had to think about how I was going to keep Judge Beck out of the house, or safely confined in his bedroom. It would be horribly awkward if I had to explain a séance to my roommate.

Everyone finished their glass of wine and slowly headed back home until it was just me, a ghost, a tray full of dirty wine glasses, and an empty bottle on my porch. On Fridays the party tended to run a little longer, but today was Thursday, and everyone had to be at work in the morning. I waved the last few neighbors goodbye and turned to pick up the tray of glasses.

The empty wine bottle tilted over and rolled off the table onto the wooden deck of my porch. Luckily the glass was thick and it didn't break. I stooped down to pick it up and tucked it under my arm as I grabbed the tray and headed for the front door.

"Stay outside," I told the ghost. "I've had enough of you tonight."

The shadow edged in beside me, and I knew that no matter how quickly I shut the door, he'd just pass through it and into my house. If only he were a vampire that had to be invited inside instead of a ghost.

Balancing the tray of glasses on one hand, I edged through the narrow door. Taco raced from the kitchen toward me. Sadly, the cat wasn't rushing to jump into my arms in a loving expression of joy at my appearance but trying to get between my legs and out the door before I managed to shut it.

I'd gotten quite good at closing the door before the cat escaped, but I knew it was just a matter of time before he squeezed through the opening. My cat was no longer confined inside, although no one would know it from his plaintive meows and the sad way he'd paw at the door. I'd taken to letting him outdoors in the enclosed cat run when I was doing yoga with Daisy, then bringing him back inside for his breakfast. I was considering doing the same thing in the evenings, giving the cat a few hours to get some fresh air. I felt guilty about not letting him roam the neighborhood, but I knew I'd still be worried sick the whole time he was out. At least with the cat run I didn't feel like I was keeping the poor thing prisoner inside my house.

Taco skidded to a halt in front of me, giving me the stink eye before turning his attention to something just behind my left shoulder. I felt a chill run through me. My cat hissed and arched his back. The chill vanished.

"Good boy," I told my cat, thrilled that he'd managed to scare Holt's ghost off, at least for now. For his reward, I led him into the kitchen and gave him a couple of the fishy-smelling treats I'd picked up on my last grocery shopping trip. Yes, Taco was fat. Yes, I was enabling him. I liked to consider it a training measure. Scare off Holt's ghost, get a fish treat.

Yanking two plates from the cupboard, I took the lid off the Crock-Pot, my mouth watering as the smell of chicken with the creamy mushroom sauce. Spooning rice onto the plates from the warmer, I ladled the chicken and sauce on top, grabbed two sets of silverware, and headed into the dining room. Judge Beck was there, as usual, papers spread everywhere.

"Dinner," I announced, carefully moving some of the papers then sliding a plate over toward him. "You can't set legal precedents on an empty stomach."

"It's less about setting it and more about finding it," he complained. With a huff of exasperation, he moved a stack of papers safely away from the plate and dug in. I sat down opposite him and did the same. For the next five minutes the only sounds were the scrapes of forks on plates and the occasional sigh of contentment. I eyed some of the papers upside-down and got an eye full of legalese.

"The kids come a week from Sunday," I broke the silence. "We should do something fun. Family movie night and pizza? A neighborhood party, or something that's just us? I can make a welcome-back cake and we can just chill."

"Chill and listen to them tell us all about the amazing cruise to the Bahamas they were on with their mom. Then they'll accidently let slip that Tyler was with them, and there will be a horrible awkward silence."

I wasn't sure how to reply to that, so I just shoved more chicken and rice into my mouth.

"I'm jealous." Judge Beck looked over at me with a wry smile. "Heather's living in our home while I'm renting a room in a house. She's taking the kids on a cruise while I barely have enough money to take them out for ice cream—not that I can take the time off work to go on vacation anyway. It's bad enough that Tyler has taken my place with my wife. Now he's stepped into my shoes with my kids."

It was the last that bothered him the most, I knew. "Madison and Henry love you. No one can ever take your place in their hearts. And, honestly, they're probably feeling a bit angry at their mother for all this. In their minds, she's ousted you from their home and is trying to replace you with some other guy. They're not going to fall for that."

He sighed. "A Bahamas cruise may change their mind.

And as much as I'd like to shove pins in a voodoo doll of Tyler, he's a nice guy. He's fun and easygoing and, unlike me, doesn't have a job where his workload eats up fourteen hours a day."

"He's not their father. And he never will be," I countered.

He shook his head. "I'll never get used to this. Not seeing my kids half the month, having them off on vacation without me. Having to celebrate their birthdays a week late because Heather has them that week and having me over for their actual birthday would be too 'awkward,' according to her."

Madison's birthday had fallen during this week, and the judge hadn't even been able to call her because they were out in the middle of the ocean. I felt for him. Really, I did.

"Could be worse, I guess." He pushed the empty plate aside. "Violet Smith called me last week wanting to see if I could exert some influence and get the folks at juvie to bend the rules so she could bring a cake and presents in for Peony's birthday."

I winced, remembering the girl was spending her sixteenth birthday in jail. If things didn't go well with her sentencing, she'd be spending a whole lot more than just the one birthday in jail, too.

"Did you? I hate the thought of her not at least having a cake."

"Me too. I doubt that girl's first fifteen birthdays were all that special, but to be in jail..." He sighed. "Rules are rules. No outside food. No gifts. Not even any outside reading material. Violet visits her regularly, so that was the girl's birthday present. Me moaning over having to wait an extra week to give Madison her gift seems petty in comparison."

Judge Beck wasn't overly fond of Peony, and he definitely wasn't thrilled about his daughter's friendship with a girl who he'd thought to be a bad influence even before she'd confessed to manslaughter, but in the last few weeks, I'd seen that he had a soft spot for all kids, even the ones who were paying for their crimes.

"How is her case going?" I asked with a quick glance around to make sure Holt's ghost hadn't returned with this topic of conversation. "Are they any closer to a plea deal? Seems like it's taking forever."

"It *is* taking forever. Holt's mother is pushing for a maximum sentence." Judge Beck slipped on his readers and pulled a stack of papers closer. "He was a high-profile figure locally, in the prime of his life with the promise of an illustrious career and future ahead of him. It doesn't look good, Kay. There's pressure to have her tried as an adult. There's pressure to prosecute this as a second-degree, or even first-degree murder instead of manslaughter. This is a case where Manifest Injustice Sentencing might apply even if her attorney gets the manslaughter deal."

My breath lodged in my throat, solid like a boulder. "But you...you get to decide that, right? The judge decides the sentencing, right?"

He looked up from his papers, peering over the reading glasses he'd finally become comfortable wearing around me. "It's not my case, Kay. Judge Stevens is presiding. And I'm glad of that because I'm not sure I even could. I know her. She's a friend of my daughter's. And you were the one who brought her in to confess. I'm too involved to judge this case."

I nodded, all the light-hearted fun of the happy hour vanishing. Judge Beck was down because of his kids and the divorce, and now I was down because of a young girl I hardly knew. Yes, she'd done wrong, but wasn't the goal of the justice system to rehabilitate and turn felons into contributing, law-abiding citizens? It was too disheartening to think that Peony might spend the rest of her childhood and most of her adult life in jail when killing someone wasn't her intent, when there were other contributing factors. It just wasn't fair.

I hated when life wasn't fair. And I was tired of having that fact rubbed in my face, from Eli's accident, to the judge's contentious divorce, to a young girl in jail.

"I've got the dishes," I said as I reached over to collect Judge Beck's plate. "You work, and I'll clean up here."

"Thanks," he mumbled, already engrossed in his papers.

I put away the leftovers and managed to get the plates into the dishwasher before Taco took the opportunity to do a little pre-cleaning of his own. That done, I headed upstairs, cat in my arms, figuring I'd call it an early night. Maybe I'd do a little knitting in bed.

Or maybe I'd read.

I put Taco on top of my comforter, then eyed the stack of paperbacks on my bedside table. Feeling as if I were crossing the point of no return, I picked them up, examining the covers. They showed lots of bare man chest with rippling abs and pecs big enough to fill out a B cup bra. A few of the book covers sported arcane symbols behind the man, looking as if they'd been branded into the dark city-scape with fire. Others had a knife between the title text with drops of red blood dripping down the blade. I chose the dog-eared one that looked like it had been read a hundred times and set the others back on the bedside table.

At four in the morning, I was still reading—and I was contemplating that cold shower. The girls had been right—this *was* steamy stuff. But the books held more than just sexy-time romance; they were well written with complex characters and they had engaging, if unbelievably fantastic, plots. I found myself on edge, unable to put the book down until I knew whether Trelanie survived the dungeon of horrors or not. I hoped Roman didn't sweep in for the rescue, wanting the woman to fight her way through the ghouls and undead to freedom unaided. I was pretty sure she was going to survive, given that this was book one of what was to be a ten--book series, but my heart still raced as I read the big battle scene.

And Roman… I'd never known such a damaged, angsty, borderline psychotic character in my life. Why was everyone wanting Trelanie to end up with this undead creep who hacked into her cell phone, stalked her when she went on dates, and even kidnapped her, all with the flimsy excuse of wanting to keep her 'safe'? I agreed with Olive: Girl needed to get a stake and go all Van Helsing on this guy. I much preferred Barton Wells, the bookish researcher who'd discovered through his studies how to inoculate against the vampirism virus and had single-handedly taken down an entire coven of evil witches—all from the confines of his wheelchair. I got the feeling that I was in the minority, though. From our conversations on the porch, it seemed that all my strong feminist friends, who would have either pepper-sprayed Roman or taken out a restraining order on him in real life, were half in love with him.

I wanted to finish it. I so wanted to power through the night and read 'the end' on this surprisingly addictive book, but the words were starting to blur together and Luanne Trainor might not appreciate me falling asleep behind the wheel when I picked her up at the airport in six short hours, so I left Trelanie in the dungeon, shouting expletives at her captors and yanking futilely on her chains, and rolled over to sleep.

CHAPTER 3

I was up early, getting in some sunrise yoga with Daisy before hauling the two hours to the airport in my car to pick up our celebrity author. I'd swung by the do-it-yourself carwash earlier in the week to give my auto a good clean-out and washing. Yes, the sedan was older than both Madison and Henry, but she was in decent shape and still had a lot of miles left in her, thanks to my frugal driving habits over the last decade. I'd still given her a quick look over before heading to the airport, just so I wouldn't be embarrassed by an inch of dust on the dashboard or the stray petrified French fry wedged between the seat and the console.

The hourly garage was packed, so I needed to park all the way at the top, then hurry to get to the airport before the plane landed. It would probably take Ms. Trainor twenty minutes or more to get off the plane and through the concourse to where I was to meet her, but I didn't want to take any chances.

I made it in plenty of time and stood in the baggage claim area, feeling like a total idiot as I held up a sign with Luanne's name in bold Sharpie. It was me and the limo drivers, eyeing every passerby expectantly. I'd seen the author's picture on the back of the books on my nightstand but didn't trust that I would recognize her. Given the amount of professional make-up, lighting, and Photoshopping that went into even the most casual social media post nowadays, there was a good chance Ms. Trainor wouldn't look anything like her picture.

It was a good thing I had the sign, because the woman that arrived in one of those motorized carts, beeping along with one of the airport staff driving, bore only a faint resemblance to the headshot I'd seen. Yes, the Luanne Trainor in front of me had long auburn hair, but instead of tamed waves it was sprayed out into a cross between '80s big hair and '70s Farrah Fawcett. The make-up that looked understated in her photo in reality seemed to have been applied with a particularly liberal trowel. Instead of an elegant A-line dress, she wore Peg Bundy leopard-print tights and a short, baggy shirt that looked as if it had been stolen from the set of *Flashdance*.

And her shoes... The author waited for the driver to assist her in climbing from the car, which was probably wise. Her glossy red pumps were on three-inch platform soles, and had pointed stiletto heels that looked to be five inches long. She was practically *en pointe*. I had no idea how she stood in those things, let alone walked.

She looked at my sign and made no move to come toward me. I noticed that the driver of the cart had gone over and spoken to another employee who was hauling an enormous roller-bag our way.

He parked the bag beside her, and as I approached, she thrust the huge roller-bag at me.

I grabbed the handle of the suitcase because the only other alternative was to let it fall onto the floor, then I shoved my sign under my arm and extended my hand. "Ms.

Trainor? I'm Kay Carrera. I'll be coordinating everything for you this weekend. It's wonderful to meet you."

She gave my hand a quick pump. "Thanks. Is your limo out front?"

Limo? Was that New York slang for any sort of car service automobile? Surely she wasn't expecting an actual limousine. We didn't have those sorts of things in Locust Point, or in Milford, for that matter. Even the kids on prom nights didn't get limousines. Brides needed to contract with car services an hour away if they wanted one.

"Um, my car is in the garage." I hesitated, looking down at her shoes—which were more like really expensive leather stilts. I doubted she could make it to the curb, let alone my car on the sixth floor of the garage. "Uh, I'll go get it and come pick you up."

She didn't say anything, and I went back and forth on whether I should haul the huge suitcase all the way to the car or leave it with her on the curb. Probably the latter.

Thankfully she followed me as I exited the airport and went the short distance to where the pick-up area was. It took a while. She didn't move very quickly in those shoes.

"Why don't you sit here?" I indicated the bench a few feet from the curb. "I'll bring the car around."

"I'm not sitting on that," she protested. "It's filthy. Do you know how much these pants cost?"

I took a deep breath and decided I couldn't trust myself to respond. No, I didn't know how much her pants cost. And yes, the bench probably was dirty, but in my opinion, it was preferable to standing around in those heels. Maybe I should have brought some of those toilet-seat covers from the airport restroom to put down on the bench for her.

Leaving the roller-bag by her side, I took off at a brisk walk across the roadway, breaking into a jog as I hit the parking garage. The elevator took forever, and it wasn't exactly easy backing my car out of the tiny parking space I'd wedged it into, but I did the best I could to limit how long Ms. Trainor had to stand around in those ridiculous shoes.

Pulling up to the curb, I hopped out to find Luanne Trainor staring with horror at my car.

"That's not…I'm not getting in that thing. I can't be seen in that."

I felt as though she'd slapped me. For a second, I wanted to cry, then I got angry. There was nothing wrong with my car. It was old, but it wasn't rusty or dented up. It was squeaky clean. And if she didn't like it, she could walk the almost hundred miles to Milford. I wasn't getting paid to do this. I'd taken the day off work and volunteered my time and gas to haul her back and forth. No way was this woman going to make me feel ashamed about my car.

"If you have a problem, then call your agent," I told her. "We don't have car companies with actual limousines in Milford or Locust Point, and my sedan is a heck of a lot cleaner and better smelling than some of the taxis around here. If you truly don't want me to drive you, then you'll need to sit here—oh, sorry, I mean *stand* here—and wait for a car service to show up that meets your standards."

The woman blinked at me in surprise. "I guess I shouldn't be so shocked that there are no limos in the sticks here. At least it's clean. I'll just wear my sunglasses and scoot down a bit so no one sees me in there."

Oh, for Pete's sake. I bit my tongue and went around to pop the trunk.

"Did my agent send you my list of dietary requirements?" she asked.

Oh, no. Here come the 'no green M&Ms' rules. Although in all fairness the woman might have a terrible peanut allergy or something. It wouldn't do to have our guest speaker going into anaphylactic shock on stage during her presentation. I made a mental note to check and make sure somebody got the list. "No, but she probably sent them to Nancy, who's taking care of the venue and the catering."

"And the inn? My agent said the choices in your little town were pretty much the Motel 6 and some Norman Bates hotel."

I was more than a bit stung by the criticism. Milford wasn't exactly Richmond-sized, but it was a real city with a nice selection of hotels. "All the chains are on the outskirts. We thought you'd want to be fairly close to the theater where you'll be speaking, so we booked your stay at Billingsly's Bed and Breakfast. It's lovely and only three blocks away."

She made no move to come toward my vehicle. "Is there a car and driver assigned to me? Or is that your job?"

Deciding she wasn't going to bring her suitcase the scant eight feet to my car, I walked over and grabbed it.

"You're in town two nights." I hefted her bag into the trunk and turned to find her behind me, extending the smaller one for me to do the same. "Is there somewhere you need to go that you'd need a car service?"

She sniffed, pushing the bag into my hands. "I do. How close is Bayforest?

Bayforest? What the heck would she need to do in Bayforest? It was even smaller than Locust Point. All that town had to its name was a church, a bakery, and a gas station.

"It's an hour from Milford." I took a deep breath. "Would you like me to take you there? Tonight? Or…" It would have to be tonight. She was booked the rest of the weekend and flying back to New York on Sunday morning. There went my séance plans with Olive and the potential late-night movie with Judge Beck.

"Maybe Sunday morning, before I fly out." She waved a hand in the air. "Oh, and I'll need a ride to the theater. I'm assuming a little town like Milbank doesn't have taxi service."

"Milford. Yes, we do have taxis, but you have to call for one and it takes about twenty minutes. You're better off calling an Uber. And the theater is three blocks from your B&B. You can walk there."

I glanced down at her shoes, hoping she'd brought some alternative footwear, or she wouldn't be walking anywhere. A surge of irritation ran through me. Maybe I wasn't the best choice of people to pick Luanne Trainor from the airport after all. Nancy should have picked someone else. I grimaced, thinking of the two-hour car ride with this detestable woman. With any luck, she'd be on her phone the whole time and I wouldn't have to actually interact with her once we were on our way. I envisioned driving up to Billingsly's and shoving her and her bag onto the curb, then peeling rubber away from there.

"I can't walk three blocks in my heels," she grumbled. "I'll need to speak to my agent about this."

Her poor agent. Did this agent even have a name? Or a gender? Whoever he—or she— was, they weren't paying this agent enough to deal with Ms. Trainor.

I slammed the trunk shut with a bit more force then necessary, then went to get into the car. I had my door open before I realized our speaker was behind me, staring at the rear door handle behind the driver's seat. Not wanting to get into an argument in the middle of the airport pick-up lane and realizing that I probably needed to make nice with this woman, I turned around and opened the door for her. Two days. Just two days and she'd be gone. I waited for her to settle herself in the back seat and closed the door, then counted to ten and took slow cleansing breaths as I got into my car and navigated out of the airport.

Once we were on the highway, I peeked in the rearview

mirror and saw her typing away on her phone. A few times she grumbled something about needing a stiff drink, and something else about stupid lawyers, stupid people with broken printers, and stupid people who couldn't get their butts to a notary. Eventually she tossed the phone onto the seat hard enough that I heard it bounce.

Maybe she was just having a horrible day and I'd caught her at the absolute worst time in her life. I found it hard to connect the author of those thrilling, steamy, insightful novels with this...unpleasant diva so I took a deep breath and vowed to give the woman a second chance.

"I'll admit I'm probably the only woman in the county who hasn't read your books," I commented, glancing at her once again through the rearview. "I started book one of your Fanged Darkness series last night and barely got any sleep. It's really good."

"Thank you. I'm glad you enjoyed it."

Could her response be any more wooden? I gritted my teeth and tried again. "I'm at the part where Trelanie is a captive in the dungeon. I know she has to live because there are supposed to be nine other books in the series before it ends, but I'm really afraid for her. You did a great job with the tension in that scene."

I could practically feel the eye roll from the back seat passenger. "Let me guess, you're an author as well and would like me to look at something you wrote and recommend it to my agent."

Unpleasant diva was beginning to seem like an understatement. How could such a horrible woman write such amazing novels?

"No, but I used to be a journalist," I told her, trying to keep my tone light and friendly. "I've got a degree in English Literature, and I read a lot. At least I used to. I'm just delivering some praise and letting you know how much I love the book so far."

"Good. Make sure you buy the rest of them because I don't make any money if you borrow them from your friends or the library."

"The library bought them somewhere," I retorted. Yes, those were Daisy's copies on my nightstand, but the woman didn't have to be such a jerk about it.

"And I'll bet you're swooning over Roman, too. He's the only reason everyone reads those books," she snarled.

Why did she sound so bitter about that? And 'those' books? Did she hate what she was doing? I knew it would be tough to be trapped into continuing a series long after the muse had left, bowing to the pressures of a publishing house, rabid fans, and the need to pay the mortgage, but from what my friends had said, book six that released last year was just as good as book one. If she was going through the motions at this point, it clearly wasn't showing in her prose—another indication that she was a very talented woman, no matter how nasty she was in person.

"I'm actually not a fan of Roman," I confessed. "Sexual prowess aside, he doesn't seem to have much going for him. I prefer Barton Wells."

Her eyes about bugged out, then a sneer twisted her lips. "Barton Wells?"

"He's smart and kind, and very brave. He lets Trelanie do her thing without the need to constantly try to save her. He doesn't do weird stalker things like break into her house and watch her sleeping, or sneak around in the bushes outside the bar watching when she's out with her friends. He respects her and admires her for her abilities and inner strength."

"Women don't want that in a man," she scoffed. "I would

have been penniless in a back alley if I'd written a series with Barton Wells as the hero and love interest."

"Probably," I agreed. "All my friends agree with you, at least as far as book boyfriends go."

"It's fantasy," she told me with a glare. "Entertainment. In real life, Roman would be in jail and he wouldn't be a vampire, either. He'd just be some good looking, controlling ass of a guy. But in a fantasy world, he's every woman's ideal man."

Not mine, but certainly Daisy's and Kat's, and Suzette's. At least when it came to fiction. But even though I wasn't particularly fond of the hero, I was enjoying the series.

"And Barton Wells?" Luanne continued. "I don't understand the vocal minority who have decided that idiot is worth any more page space then he already has gotten. I'm sorry I ever put him in the book."

"Well, I'm not," I retorted. Then I realized I needed to be nice to this woman and dialed it back a bit. "I like Barton Wells. And although I think Roman is kind of...intense, I like him too. I like all the characters you've written. You're very talented and deserve your success."

"I do deserve it. I deserve every dime of that money. Every dime," Luanne grumbled. "I'm happy to cash my checks every six months. Although I wish it had been one of my other series that had taken off instead of these two."

"You wrote other novels?" I asked in surprise. "Were they in a different genre? Literary fiction? Poetry?" She was clearly a talented storyteller, but LitFic and Poetry had a smaller audience and there was quite a bit of competition in discoverability. No wonder she was bitter if those far more difficult novels bombed where the lighter genre ones took off.

"No, my other books were fantasy novels as well." She picked her phone up off the seat. "They're better than Fanged

Darkness or Infernal Awakenings. Far better. There's no accounting for taste, I guess."

I was far from fond of Luanne Trainor from what I'd experienced of her so far, but I did feel a tiny bit of sympathy for her at this. I couldn't imagine how frustrating it would be to have written a series that came from your heart, only to have the one you felt was of lesser value take off.

"Were those other books written under your name?" I asked, determined to go seek them out. I thought that first Fanged Darkness book was amazing, so I was sure these other books would knock my socks off.

"Yes." She typed on her phone, clearly distracted. "Broken Wolf Series and Witches Gone Wild. The publisher didn't want to pick up anything after book two, but I insisted. And since Infernal Awakenings and Fanged Darkness regularly hit the New York Times list, they capitulated. Didn't mean they put the slightest bit of marketing behind them. Do you know they only authorized a five thousand book print run? I was outraged."

"Well…that's terrible." I wasn't sure what to say. Five thousand sounded like a lot to me, but what did I know? Obviously, it was far less than what the other series got, but if they weren't selling, then the publisher obviously wouldn't want to risk the money on a huge print run. But whose fault was that? If the publisher never got behind the books with adequate marketing, no wonder they flopped. It seemed like a bit of a chicken-or-egg scenario.

Luanne Trainor didn't respond, and we spent the rest of the trip in silence, the only sound the occasional tap-tap of her fingers on the phone. When we entered Milford, I pointed out a few of the interesting local sites, and she ignored me, not even grunting in acknowledgement. So much for my attempts to play the tour guide.

We pulled up in front of the B&B, and although I was

tempted to leave Ms. Trainor at the curb, I owed it to Nancy to do my best to make this guest feel welcome. Putting the car in park, I opened the back door for our guest, then headed to the rear of the car to wrestle her luggage out of the trunk. Then I led the way to the front door, struggling a bit with the suitcase over the brick walkway and up the porch stairs. Looking back, I saw Luanne was struggling even more than I was, her pointy-heeled, lofty shoes wobbling around as if they were on the verge of causing the woman to break an ankle.

After she managed to make her way up the steps, I went for the door, holding it open as she clacked her way over the threshold. Gene Billingsly greeted us just inside the foyer, welcoming us with a beaming smile. I signed the paperwork and turned Luanne Trainor over to him, telling her that I'd see her tomorrow morning for the reader's brunch, and to let me know if there was anything she needed.

I hoped she didn't need anything else. I'd expected she'd want to rest after the flight and prepare for the full day tomorrow, but her weird request to drive to Bayforest threw me. For all I knew, she'd want me to stay at the inn all night and haul her around town like a chauffeur.

"You have my dietary requirements?" Luanne ignored me and glared at the innkeeper.

Gene's smile never faltered. "Of course! Ms. Zinovi made sure to send us a copy. I can assure you that we have a special breakfast prepared just for you, and we've also arranged for several local restaurants to deliver meals in accordance with your specifications. Don't worry, Ms. Trainor. Everything has been taken care of."

Gene Billingsly was a saint. As was his wife, Paula, whom I'm sure had slaved over whatever dietary requirements Luanne had in an effort to make the woman's stay perfect. That was the sort of people they were, and one of the reasons

Nancy liked to use their adorable inn for speakers at the theater.

I thanked Gene and turned to leave, grinning a bit as I heard him tell Luanne how much his wife, Paula, had loved the series, and that she hoped the rumors of a film deal were true. Hopefully neither of them would ask about Barton Wells. Or expect Luanne to carry her own luggage.

CHAPTER 4

It was two in the afternoon by the time I made it back to my house. I'd never been so exhausted before. Driving Luanne Trainor had been a most unpleasant experience. My only hope was that this facet of her personality was a temporary funk and she'd be able to shake it off before the brunch tomorrow morning. If not, this was going to be a very long weekend.

Taco did his usual race for the door when I entered, skidding to a halt and glaring at me as I quickly shut it behind my back. I'd missed lunch, so I made myself a ham and swiss sandwich and fed him a few bits of ham as a consolation for having to stay in the house. He'd sulked in his enclosed pen this morning while Daisy and I were doing our yoga and had given me the stink-eye until I'd fed him breakfast. I didn't want to take a chance on letting him out mid-afternoon like this, especially on a Friday when early commuter traffic was liable to send more cars than usual down our normally quiet roads. Later I'd put him in the cat run, although I was beginning to think that solution wasn't any better in Taco's eyes than being cooped up inside.

I was gathering my ingredients for my special contribution to the food at the meet-and-greet when Nancy called and launched straight into a stress-filled narrative.

"The agent arrived and I'm trying to work with the lighting and sound guy for the extra mics and there's an extra thirty tickets we managed to squeeze out by opening up the balcony seating a bit. Oh, and can you swing by and pick up the programs at the printer on your way in to the brunch tomorrow?"

"Hi, Nancy. How nice to hear from you," I teased. "Our author has been transported safely to Billingsly's and into Gene and Paula's hands. And of course I'll pick up the programs for you. Is there anything else I can do to help?"

"Just make sure Luanne Trainor is on time for the brunch. These people paid a lot for that event. I want to make sure they feel they're getting their money's worth. Paula's going to put on an amazing spread, and I've got flowers arriving for the table, and little giveaways for the attendees with a signed book and some little freebie things like bookmarks, magnets, and tote bags that the agent brought from the publisher." Nancy paused and took a - much-needed breath. "Oh, Kay, I'm so scared something is going to go wrong. We don't get big name speakers like this around here. I can't believe Luanne Trainor actually agreed to come to our little town like this. What if something goes wrong?"

"Nothing is going to go wrong," I soothed her. Then I remembered our guest of honor. "Have you...do you know anything about Luanne Trainor personally? Does she do a lot of these sorts of things?"

"No. She usually refuses to do anything besides brief appearances at large, national conferences. These small venue things aren't normally her thing, which is why I was so shocked when she agreed to come. Why?" Nancy's voice hitched. "Did something happen on the ride from the airport?"

"No. It's just..." I hesitated, not wanting to add to Nancy's stress, but also not wanting her to be blindsided tomorrow at the brunch if her author guest wasn't exactly what she'd expected. "Luanne Trainor doesn't seem to have very good social skills from my brief experience in driving her from the airport. Maybe she's just not good one-on-one. Maybe she's fine in larger groups, or she'll treat it as a performance or something. She just...she wasn't very nice."

I had a lot of stronger words I wanted to use to describe Luanne Trainor but didn't feel they were either ladylike or appropriate to say over the phone to Nancy.

"Oh, no." Nancy's voice squeaked. "Is she going to cause a scene? Insult someone? We can't cancel the brunch at this late date."

"I'm sure it will be fine," I told her. "Maybe the agent will help steer the conversation and keep Luanne in check. There's nothing either of us can do about the woman's personality. We'll just hope for the best and go on with it. I shouldn't have said anything, but I wanted you to know that she's kind of...prickly."

Nancy muttered something about spiking the author's coffee if that would help, then voiced her appreciation for my assistance before hanging up. I shook my head and sat my phone on the counter, feeling sorry for my friend. Two days. Two days and Luanne Trainor would be gone, and Nancy would be basking in the glow of having managed to bring a big name to the theater's speaker series—a series that usually only attracted the occasional college professor or local historian. I think the closest thing we'd had to a best-selling author in the last decade had been that environmentalist out of Richmond who'd written a book about the changes in saltwater marshes over the last century.

It would all be fine. That agent woman would help keep Luanne from offending anyone, and I'd do my best as well. Two days.

But in the meantime, I had an icebox cake to prepare.

A dozen eggs. A pound of softened butter. Powdered sugar, cocoa, baking chocolate, and real vanilla. I'd bought ladyfingers earlier in the week, knowing that I wouldn't have time to make them myself. Looking around to make sure Taco wasn't lurking nearby, ready to leap on the counter and grab either the ladyfingers or a stick of butter, I got started separating the eggs.

Icebox cake was one of my favorite desserts, but it was a gazillion calories of rich, decadent goodness. Basically, thick layers of alternating vanilla and chocolate buttercream icing separated with ladyfingers and chilled, it was often requested at holiday parties and special occasions. This was a special occasion. Nancy had caterers who would be providing all the other food for the meet-and-greet, but she'd asked for me to make this. I knew it was her favorite. The poor woman was so stressed she deserved a dessert made with a pound of butter. I'd have to make sure I set aside some for her before the rest of the attendees devoured it all.

Once I'd finished the icebox cake, I whipped up some mini meatloaves and stuck them in the oven for dinner, then eyed the clock. The judge should be home in another hour or two. My plan was to ply him with meatloaf and au gratin potatoes, then make up some excuse why he had to go up to his room at nightfall and not come out for a few hours. Olive was due over then, and I didn't really want the judge discovering that we had a ghost problem in the house, and that I was able to see them. Although Holt had been fairly quiet today. There'd been no additional poltergeist activity since happy hour on the porch last night. Maybe he'd decided to behave himself. Maybe he'd decided to go haunt his mother instead, and Olive, the judge, and I could all just sit around the table and eat pie or something.

I heard the clatter of a wooden spoon hitting the floor and took a breath, turning around to scold the ghost I'd hoped had vanished forever, only to see Taco up on the countertop, happily licking the bowl I'd used to stir up the meatloaf.

"I just fed you," I scolded, scooping him up and depositing him on the floor. With an angry *meow,* he hopped right back up on the counter, squeezing between my arms to shove half his body into the bowl and nearly falling into the sink in the process. With a sigh, I let him have the bowl, bending down to pick up the spoon and drop it in the sink. He was fat in spite of my attempts to limit his food and treats, and this sort of thing was the reason why. A licked bowl here, a dropped potato chip there, and adoring children who were constantly slipping him little bits of their food. No wonder he was pudgy. And I suspected that Judge Beck was doing the same in spite of his protests to the contrary.

Leaving Taco to his pre-wash efforts, I headed into the parlor and opened up my laptop. Luanne Trainor's novels were easy to find on the e-book distributor, but row after row were filled with Infernal Awakenings and Fanged Darkness—e-books, paperbacks, hardbacks, used books from various sellers, audio editions, a gazillion different licensed merchandise items from Trelanie and Roman salt and pepper shakers to a naughty accessories kit, no doubt to reenact those spicy scenes from the book.

Ten pages back I finally found book one of the Broken Wolf series. I downloaded it, then searched another four pages of products before I found book one of Witches Gone Wild. I curled up on the couch with a blanket and the laptop. Done with his bowl-licking, Taco trotted in to join me, exhaling his ground-beef breath in my face as I opened the first in the Broken Wolf series and tucked in for an hour of reading enjoyment.

Ten pages in and I was on the internet, searching to see if there wasn't some other author named Luanne Trainor who'd published this book. Then I went back to the sales page just to make sure this was her book and not some imposter. Then I checked the date, wondering if she'd written this very early in her career.

Yeah. It was that bad. The characters were wooden stereotypes, the dialogue stilted. The plot was unrealistic, even for a fantasy series with werewolves, and the descriptions went on and on until I felt like throwing my computer against the wall. It was nothing like her more popular series. Nothing. I couldn't believe the same person wrote these books, but according to the distribution site and the publisher's information, Luanne Trainor was the author of all four series. Clearly she'd had some sort of talent epiphany about ten years ago.

I stroked Taco's head, pushing his big furry body a bit to the side and opened up Witches Gone Wild, thinking that this series might show the link, the progression in writing skill between Broken Wolf and Fanged Darkness. It was equally horrible. In all honesty, it probably wasn't *horrible*. It was okay. It was average. It wasn't any different than the million other fantasy novels out there. It was when I compared it to the incredible book I'd read last night that these two novels seemed horrible. Pushing Taco off my lap, I set my laptop on the coffee table and headed upstairs to bring down the Fanged Darkness book I'd been reading. Within seconds, I was lost in the world of Trelanie and Roman, trapped in that dungeon with her, using the sharp edge of the stone to pry open the links of her chains and wrench her bloodied wrists free. By the time I heard Judge Beck's key in the lock, I was glued to the page, holding my breath as Trelanie battled ghouls and blood-crazed vampires with the chain that had once held her wrists, screaming vengeance like a Valkyrie. Judge Beck called a hello and I held up a finger, unable to pay any attention to him until Trelanie had managed to escape the dungeon into the brilliant sunlight where no creature of darkness dared follow.

"I take it that's not Great Expectations," the judge drawled, gesturing toward the cover of my paperback which featured a naked male torso, his head and nether regions unfairly cut off by the size limits of the cover.

"Fanged Darkness," I told him. "Research, you know. It's important for me to have some familiarity with Luanne Trainor's novels if I'm going to be the speaker's liaison."

A slow grin creased his face, his blue eyes dancing. "Ah. Excellent excuse, Kay. I'd totally believe it if I hadn't seen all those romance novels on the bookshelf downstairs."

I laughed. "Okay, you've got me. I'm not the literary snob you probably initially took me for. I've always been a fan of romance novels, although I'll admit that these vampire/demon/werewolf ones are a new guilty pleasure. There's a lot more going on than just the romance. Trelanie is battling an ancient family curse and trying to live up to her legacy as the holder of the Whip of Destiny."

"Whip of Destiny." Judge Beck snorted.

"It's a dual-purpose whip," I told him, struggling to keep a straight expression on my face. "Beats down the bad guys, but when the lights go down…"

"Boom-chicka-wow-wow?" he repeated Daisy's term.

"Yes, there's a whole lot of boom-chicka-wow-wow, both with and without the Whip of Destiny."

There was a split second of silence, then the pair of us burst into laughter.

"I've got meatloaf in the oven," I told him, wiping my eyes.

"And potatoes au gratin. We can throw together a salad as well, if you like."

"I'll get the salad and check on the food," he told me. "You stay here and finish your chapter. I don't want you to leave your girl Trelanie in...in the middle of things."

He gave me a saucy wink and headed into the kitchen, whistling to himself.

It was nice to sit back and read while someone else took care of dinner. Judge Beck popped his head in to let me know when it was all ready and I set my book aside and went to find the dining room set with my nice china, the food in elegant serving dishes and the salad in crystal.

"Are we celebrating?" I laughed.

"It's Friday. You've got a busy weekend with your author guest in town. The kids are gone for another week." The judge nodded. "I figured we both needed a fancy dinner tonight."

He pulled a chair out for me, and we ate meatloaf in style, drinking water in wine glasses, with cloth napkins draped across our laps. The judge told me about his day, about his plans for golf tomorrow, and talked excitedly about what he wanted to do for Madison's belated birthday celebration. I told him all about Luanne Trainor and we laughed about the woman's absurd footwear. After dinner, we carried in the dishes, and I got to work on rinsing and stacking while Judge Beck put the leftovers away. It was a wonderful evening. But then again, all the evenings I'd had with the judge and his family had been wonderful.

"So, ice cream and a movie?" he asked, peering into the freezer to survey our options. "It's Friday night. Let's not spend it with our work spread across the dining room table. Let's get fat and lazy and binge watch an entire season of Law and Order or something."

I grimaced, feeling a bit guilty for what I was about to say.

"Umm, maybe late tonight? Or Sunday? Olive is coming over around ten for an hour or two. She's got some…some girl stuff she wants to talk to me about."

"Oh." Judge Beck shut the freezer door. "So I need to be out of your hair then, I guess. Are you guys going to be downstairs, or up here? I'm assuming this is 'girl stuff' that's not meant for my ears."

I was both grateful that he caught on quickly and bummed that I was turning him down for ice-cream-and-movie-binge activities. "We're probably going to be in the dining room."

He smiled. "So, am I confined to my bedroom, or am I safe to go downstairs and watch TV? How long is the 'girl stuff' conversation going to last? Will I be able to emerge from my cave sometime around midnight, or do you foresee this private conversation going on all night?"

He was teasing. It made me feel better about all this that he seemed okay with being shooed away from half of the house he was paying money to live in.

"Probably no more than an hour or so," I assured him. "How about I come get you downstairs when we're done?"

"Sounds like a plan. Do you think Olive would want to join in on some Law and Order binging?"

I chuckled. "Maybe. I'll ask her."

"In that case, I'll leave you to your book." He looked back at me as he headed out of the kitchen. "Thanks for dinner. Sunday it's my turn to cook though, okay?"

"Deal." I watched him go with a smile on my face. I loved having him live here with me. Yes, I adored the kids, but there was something special about the weeks when it was just me and the judge. Something special indeed.

CHAPTER 5

Olive arrived promptly at nine o'clock, hauling a gorgeous leather portmanteau in one hand and her designer purse in the other. We got settled at the table with some coffee as Judge Beck retreated downstairs. As soon as she heard the door shut, Olive opened the leather bag, pulling candles, incense, and a few bulky velvet bags from the inside.

"You should just tell him, you know," she told me. "He won't think you're crazy if you let him know."

"Because everyone accepts the idea that their landlord sees ghosts and that the house they're living in is haunted by her deceased husband and a young football player he wasn't very fond of before his death?"

"More people see ghosts than you'd think, Kay." She walked around the room, placing candles here and there on top of folded squares of aluminum foil to safeguard my furniture against the melted wax. "Sometimes it's just one time and they think it's a dream. Others see them regularly but ignore them and come up with some other explanation for their experiences. Some see shadows as you do. Others see the person as they appeared in life. Some can hear their voices. Some can't."

Ugh, I was glad I didn't have to hear Holt yammering about, although if I could hear him speak, maybe he'd stop knocking stuff off counters and shelves all the time. Then I thought about Eli, about how wonderful it would be to actually see *him* instead of a shadow, to hear his voice again.

Olive scooted a candle over a few inches and shot me a perceptive glance. "Would you like me to contact the other ghost as well?"

I hesitated, not sure *what* I wanted. What if I found out the ghost wasn't Eli? That the ghost was some former resident of the house from the last century and not my husband?

And what if it was Eli, and with Olive's voice he told me of all the things I'd done wrong in the last decade, all the times I'd been too tired to give him that little extra, the times I'd secretly resented having to care for him. The times I'd felt sorry for myself. All those fleeting thoughts and feelings I'd kept to myself while struggling to be the sole source of comfort for a patient who, most of the time, bore no resemblance to the man I'd married. Maybe he'd seen those thoughts and had been hurt by them. Maybe he was staying around just to tell me what a horrible wife I'd been.

No. That wasn't the feeling I got from the spirit at all. I could tell Holt's ghost was angry and frustrated, but the one I'd come to associate with Eli was just…there. He was calm and comforting, just a reassuring presence around my home when I needed it the most. No, what I really feared was that Olive would give voice to whatever Eli had to say, then he'd move on and I'd never see him again. I couldn't bear that. Losing him in the accident, then losing him this spring were difficult enough. Losing the last shadowy reminder of his presence would be too much.

"Let's just concentrate on the younger ghost today," I told

Olive. Maybe someday I'd feel ready to let Eli go, to exchange whatever words needed to still be said, then let his spirit fly free. That day wasn't today.

"Then that's what we'll do," she replied with a kind smile.

I watched her align the candles, then set two incense burners on little ceramic trays with a bit of charcoal and tiny bags of herbs and resin beside them. Then she opened the largest velvet bag and removed a mirror.

"Touching up the lipstick before we begin?" I teased. "I'm sure a ladies' man like Holt appreciates that sort of thing."

Olive laughed. "Sometimes I have to break out all the tricks. We got lucky with your last spirit. She was eager to communicate, although she had a difficult time getting her message across. Who knows how this one will react to my call?"

I looked around the room and shivered. "He's been poltergeisting stuff. And I feel like he's angry."

Olive held up the incense. "This ought to cool his jets a bit. And I have some personal precautions in case he decides he wants to take that anger out on me."

I felt suddenly ashamed that I'd never considered Olive's safety during these sessions. "We don't have to do this if you think you'll be in danger," I told her. Sheesh, it's not like I was even paying her for this. *Should* I pay her for this? The thought had never crossed my mind, but I assumed she charged a fee for these sorts of things, just as she would for her accounting services.

She chuckled. "Girl, I've had a Civil War Lieutenant try to toss me through a window, a Senator's son try to permanently possess me, and a prostitute's daughter who wanted me to kill her mother. There's nothing this football-boy could do that will faze me."

"He might knock some vegetables off the counter," I teased. "Or dump Taco's food bowl over. He only did that once, though. Taco generally avoids ghosts, but one of them messes with his food bowl, and it's game-on."

"Ghosts should know better than to mess with cats," she told me with a grin. "Now, what exactly do you want from this young man? Is there something in particular you want him to tell you? If he consents to me channeling for him, you can ask him directly, but if not, I may need to just be a go-between."

I shrugged. "The usual. Why is he still here? Why is he attaching himself to me and my house in particular? What can I do to get rid of him?"

She snorted. "Well, the last question is a bit combative so I might need to rephrase that one." She got up and adjusted the candles once more, setting each one to light while muttering under her breath in a language I couldn't recognize.

"Is he here now?" I hadn't seen either of my shadow residents for a few hours. It would suck if Holt in particular had fled the scene before Olive could wrangle him into a conversation.

"Yes." Her breath came out in a cloud of steam, as if it were suddenly fifty degrees colder on her side of the room. I sat in silence and watched her finish with the candles, then leaned forward as she positioned herself at the table, spreading her fingers wide on the surface until only her thumbs touched. A shadow appeared against the wallpaper, faint but present.

"Come on out, Holt Dupree," Olive called, dispensing with any theatrics. "I know you've got something to say, and Kay would like a word with you as well."

The shadow against the wall quivered but stayed put. I had an instant vision of Holt crossing his arms and giving us a sullen stare.

Olive took a deep breath and let it out with a whoosh. "I

feel you over there. Come talk to us. Either through me, or with the mirror. I'll even get the Ouija board out if you prefer."

I got the impression Holt didn't even know what a Ouija board was. Young people. Sheesh.

The shadow shimmered with irritation. The mirror in front of Olive frosted over, then a series of words appeared across the surface. They weren't the sort of words someone should use in polite company.

"Well." Olive laughed and shook her head. "Never had anyone call me that before, and I've been called a lot of things." She wiped her sleeve across the mirror. "How about something constructive, Holt? Or at least something without profanity."

The shadow shimmered again, and the mirror frosted, this time revealing two words, all in capital letters.

"Think it's time to put the mirror away," Olive muttered, sliding it back into the velvet bag. Shifting in her chair, she lit the incense cone and breathed deep. "Use me, Holt. But I swear, if you take the Lord's name in vain, I'm gonna banish you to the county dump for six months."

I bit back a smile, knowing that she couldn't do that but still appreciating the threat.

The shadow moved forward into the curl of incense, then hovered around Olive's shoulder. She held very still then slowly shifted her hand to the left, turning the palm upward and wiggling her fingers as if coaxing a particularly skittish kitten to come closer.

He brushed against her hand then darted back to the wall, extinguishing two candles on his way.

Olive sighed. "Almost had him."

"He's angry," I told her.

"He's afraid," she replied. "He doesn't know me, and he hasn't been a ghost for long. I feel kinda sorry for the kid, you know? But scared ghosts are the hardest ones to communicate with. Angry is better."

Angry is better, huh?

"Holt!" I called out. "I didn't like you much when you were alive, and I'm even less fond of you dead," I called out. "Peony's in jail awaiting trial or a plea deal. Buck's been charged and is out on bail. What more do you want from me? It's not like I can bring you back to life or anything."

The two candles ignited, the plume of incense smoke jutting to the left.

"You were a lousy son, and a lousy boyfriend. If you hadn't been good at football, then no one would have wanted to be your friend," I told him. "And you weren't even that good at football. Buck Stanford should have gotten that scholarship, not you. If you hadn't died on that road last month, you would have been knifed by a jealous husband and cut from the team by the end of the season. You're a jerk. I don't like you. Taco doesn't like you. You're not welcome here. So either talk to me, or get the heck out of my house."

Olive gasped and sat back in her chair with a snap, her eyes going wide.

"No bad language." I shook my finger at Olive, letting Holt know that I wasn't going to tolerate any of the nastiness that had appeared on the mirror.

"It's not fair," Olive told me. Or rather, Holt told me. Her voice had changed, becoming deeper and raspy with a slangy edge to it.

"That you're dead?" I asked. "I know it's not fair. Kids die. Infants die. Talented surgeons who are loving husbands and pillars of their community get hit by oncoming cars and are permanently disabled. Life isn't fair, Holt. Death isn't fair, either."

"I had my whole life ahead of me," he insisted. "And you don't know shi...squat about football. I was good—really good. What happened to Buck was an accident, no matter what anyone says. I was the best in high school, the best in college, and I would have brought Atlanta to the Super Bowl in a few years, I promise you that. It's not fair."

I noticed that he didn't mention the women or the fast cars or the money and fame. Maybe I had read Holt wrong. Maybe he had been passionate about his sport and *that* had been what mattered to him most—which made his death even more tragic. Even so, there was nothing I could do to help him with that.

"I'm sorry, Holt. I know you're angry, and believe me, I know how that feels. I've beat my fists against the walls for many years over the injustice of things, over how one second can change a life—change several lives—in a blink. I don't understand what this has to do with me, though."

Olive blinked up at me, her eyes boring into mine. "You were there."

I caught my breath, knowing he meant there, at the site of the accident. "I was. So were a lot of other people. Peony. The man you nearly ran off the road. The paramedics."

"If Buck hadn't fu..messed with my car, I wouldn't have wrecked. And if that bi…girl hadn't drugged my water, I would have walked away from that accident with some stitches and bruises."

"And if you hadn't been popping Viagra like they were Tic-Tacs, you wouldn't have died either way." I glared at Olive-Holt. "What's a young guy like you need that stuff for anyway? You're so concerned about your football career, but you're taking erectile dysfunction meds?"

Olive squirmed. I got the feeling that if she hadn't had a coffee-colored complexion, she would have been blushing bright red. "That's not your business. I had a prescription. It's not something I like to discuss with anyone, you know?"

Ugh. Poor kid. I couldn't imagine how embarrassing it

would have been to have *those* problems as a young man. But that wasn't my problem. None of this was my problem.

"What do you want, Holt?" I asked.

"I want my life. I was cheated out of my life and I want it back."

I couldn't really blame him for that, but what he wanted was impossible.

"Holt, I'm not a necromancer. This isn't some late-night horror movie where I can raise you from the dead or go back in time and stop everything that caused your death. I know you want your life back, but it isn't going to happen. It's not fair. I know it's not fair, but there aren't any do-overs that I'm aware of."

He sat there, sullen. It was odd because Olive was sitting right in front of me, but I could tell it wasn't her. Her mannerisms, her speech patterns...it was all Holt.

"I don't want to go."

Now my heart was breaking a little. He'd been a cocky flirt, who'd quite possibly deliberately hurt a competitor to get ahead, but he'd died young. Not even in the prime of his life. He'd died before the prime of his life could even start.

"I know," I told him softly. "But ghosts can't play football. All you can do is roll potatoes off my counter and smash a wine glass or two. We can't even communicate outside of what we're doing now. If you stay, you'll just be a shadow that only I can see—a shadow that can occasionally move something physical. What kind of life is that?"

He slumped, picking at his cuticles. I was pretty sure Olive wasn't going to be thrilled at what he was doing to her manicure. "I don't want to be dead."

It was like talking to...well, like talking to a teenager. If I couldn't convince him to head toward the light, then maybe I could at least get him to go haunt someone else.

"Why me, Holt? I know you said I was there, but so were

a lot of other people. And there must be someone you'd rather spend your afterlife with than a sixty-year-old widow that you had met in passing once or twice in your life."

"You can see me," he replied. "Maybe not all the way, but at least you know I'm around. Do you know how frustrating it is to see your mom crying and you can't touch her or talk to her? And she doesn't even know you're there watching her heart break?"

I rolled my eyes. "Holt, you hardly saw your mother when you were back for the Fourth. Be honest, it's Violet you're trying to haunt. And you're frustrated because she doesn't even know you're there or seem to care."

Olive/Holt's mouth set into a tight line. "The only people who can see me are you, a few of the homeless down on South Street in Milford, and this woman I'm talking through. I don't wanna go. And I want to be somewhere that I'm noticed."

I was tempted to tell him to go hang out on South Street, but I wasn't that cruel. "Holt, I've already got one ghost in the house. He's welcome to stay here all the time. You…well, I don't mind you visiting every now and then, but you can't stay here every day, and you can't keep following me around."

The look that Olive/Holt gave me was heartbreaking. I was so tempted to give in, but I couldn't adopt every stray ghost that came around.

"Let's work out a visitation plan or something," I told him. "For the short term. Until you decide you want to move on to the afterlife."

His eyes met mine. "Really?"

"I don't know how thrilling it's going to be for you. You can't talk to me. You're just a shadow in the corner of my vision. And I don't exactly live an exciting life. I'm a widow.

My idea of fun is reading or watching movies or petting my cat."

He shuddered at the mention of my cat.

"Your job is interesting. I can read the files you're working on and see what you're doing. I like watching you find deadbeats and research people. You're nosy. I'm nosy... or I *was* nosy before I got dead. It's better than hanging out on South Street and watching a bunch of guys beg change off the commuters."

"So how about this: you can hang out with me at work, or when I'm doing work-related activities. My social time is off the table. No hovering around during porch happy hour. No lurking while I'm cooking dinner or knitting or hanging with Judge Beck or my friends." I suddenly thought of something else. "And absolutely no following Madison around. I better not catch you in her bedroom or prowling around when she's in the shower. Got it?"

He grinned. "Aw, come on. She's a tall drink of water, that girl is."

I glared at him. "She's just turned sixteen. I mean it, Holt. I find out you're being a creepy stalker ghost and I'll.... I'll sic Taco on you."

He shuddered. "Okay, okay. Just not the cat. Work only. But if you're working from home, or something work-like comes up when you're hanging with your friends, then I get to be there. And I want to visit the barbeques. The homeless on South Street don't have barbeques."

Why did I get the feeling this ghost was going to turn a whole lot of things into "work-related" occurrences? Holt had a bit of a con man in him, and I knew full well that I couldn't trust him to keep to the spirit of our agreement. It was a starting point, though. And hopefully once he realized how very boring my life was, he'd move toward the light.

"We have a deal," I told him. "Now scoot so Olive can get

back to her own life here. I'll expect to see you at work on Monday—and not a minute before then. Got it?"

He grinned. "Got it."

Olive jerked, her eyes rolling back in her head and her hands clenching in a spasm on top of the table. The candles blew out. The incense curled then drifted lazily up to the ceiling.

"Well. That young man is very intense." Olive shook her head, then patted her hair. "Don't trust him to keep his word. He's not a bad kid, he's just…naughty. And he'll take advantage of every opportunity that comes his way. He's one of those 'better to ask forgiveness then permission' types, and I'm not sure he'll even beg forgiveness when he's done."

"Sure you can't just banish him?" I asked.

She laughed. "I think you can handle him just fine on your own, Kay. I'm gonna leave my mirror here, just in case there's something he really needs to say to you. He knows how to use it, but it might not be all that easy for him to communicate with it when I'm not here."

I watched as she pulled the mirror from her bag and set it on the table. "I'm not sure I want to use it if all I'm going to see is a bunch of profanity on a frosted surface."

"That's true. Just keep it in a drawer out of the way and only use it in emergencies." Olive got up and looked around before stuffing the mirror in the silverware drawer of the sideboard.

"I really appreciate you doing this," I told her. "What's your fee? I really feel like I should be paying you for your time and effort."

She waved her hand at me, then paused and scowled down at her chipped polish before answering. "No worries, girl. I'm glad Daisy introduced us. I've made a lot of new friends coming here to your happy hours and barbeques. Besides, it's nice to do something that doesn't involve auditing month-end reports and balance sheets. Someday I'll need a favor. How about that?"

"Well, I'll definitely owe you more than one favor. And we're all thrilled to have you in our circle of friends." I stood up as Olive gathered her things together. "I'll see you tomorrow night at the theater, right?"

"I can't wait," she replied. "Suzette and I are going to grab some dinner then head there. We're both excited to see Luanne Trainor in person. I'm hoping we get a chance to actually speak to her at the meet-and-greet as well."

I grimaced. "Well, don't get too excited. I drove her in from the airport and she's a real diva. She's not the nicest person I've ever met in my life."

Olive wrinkled her nose. "Really? That's a darned shame. I still like her books, though. It's a bucket list item for me to meet her. I guess if she says something mean to me, I can brag about it. Insulted by a famous person. How many people can lay claim to that?"

I laughed as we headed to the door, thinking how Olive was so good at finding the positive in all things. "That's true. And after today, I can cross that one off my own bucket list."

I waved Olive goodbye and watched as she got into the car and pulled out of my driveway, then I went back inside, scooped up Taco and headed downstairs. Judge Beck was sprawled across my sofa, watching old Law and Order reruns. He paused the show and went to fix us both a bowl of ice cream.

We shared the afghan that Eli's mother had made us for our wedding. Taco curled up against my leg, snoozing. The only sounds were the clink of spoons in our bowls, the television, and Taco's occasional soft rumbling purr. No ghosts. Just a quiet evening among the living.

Around midnight, we took our bowls upstairs and said our good nights. As I curled up in my cool sheets, Taco at the foot of my bed, I saw the faint shadow of a ghost materialize in the corner of my room.

"Don't leave," I told Eli. "Don't leave me. I'm not ready for you to leave me."

The shadow moved closer to the bed.

"I miss you. I'm happy, you know? I love having Judge Beck and the kids here, and I can't imagine life without Taco. My friends are wonderful. My job just gets more and more interesting. I wish you were here to share it all with."

The shadow shimmered, fading slightly.

"If that's what you're here for, then know I'll be okay," I whispered. "I love you. I'll always love you, but I'll be okay. I'll be happy. I'll have a good life. If you need to go, I'll understand. I don't want to force you to stay here when you're ready to leave. But if you could stay just a little bit longer..." I took a deep breath and forced back the tears. "I still need you, Eli. I'll always want and need you. I'm just not ready for you to go yet. Not yet."

The shadow vanished, but as I closed my eyes, I caught a scent of citrus and spice that had been Eli's favorite body wash. It lulled me to sleep, dreaming of him beside me, of his arms around me, dreaming of a time before the accident changed everything in both of our lives.

CHAPTER 6

The brunch was at noon, but I got going early to pick up the programs at the printer. I showed up at the B&B at ten, just to make sure Luanne had everything she needed and was hopefully out of bed. Nancy had texted me over the list of the author's dietary requirements, so as a peace offering, I'd picked up a large organic free-trade green tea with a splash of almond milk.

"She's still in bed," Paula Billingsly told me as I entered the dining area. She had a crisp white apron over her lavender floral-print dress. Her silver hair was held neatly back with an ornate clip. The slight tint of pink on her lips was the only makeup she wore. No nail polish or rings decorated her fingers. No jewelry adorned her neck. Only the smallest of diamond studs pierced her earlobes. Paula always looked like she should be the hostess of a cooking show, whipping up complicated meringues and custards all while appearing as fresh and as clean as a daisy in spring.

As I watched, she nudged the silverware on the huge table prepared for the brunch, ensuring each was the exact distance from the table edge and plate—whatever that distance might be. She looked…haggard, which wasn't like Paula at all.

"How'd last night go?" I asked, fearing the worst.

"Oh, let's see…had to change her sheets because the thread count was sub-par. Which was kind of funny because the ones I ended up putting on her bed were the exact same thread count as the ones that were originally on it. Then the almond cookies I sent up as a bed-time treat weren't acceptable, even though I made gluten free ones specifically for her because Nancy told me she had some special diet." Tears sparked in Paula's eyes. "I made them special. Tried three different recipes last week to make sure I'd found a good one. Had to order the nut flours off the internet and have them overnighted in because I couldn't find anywhere in Milford that sold them."

I suddenly felt the urge to stab Luanne Trainor through her nasty little heart. "Do you still have some?" I held up the coffee I'd gotten when I'd picked up Luanne's tea. "I could use a little something to go with my dark roast here."

She sniffed and motioned for me to follow her into the kitchen. All the ingredients were neatly arranged for her to begin cooking the brunch—eggs, chopped vegetables, skillets, and a tray of sliced ham covered with plastic wrap.

Paula slid a plate over toward me. The cookies were perfectly shaped hearts—the edges sharp and clean. In the middle of each was a dab of what looked like white icing in an intricate design.

"It's Roman's sigil." She pointed at the white. "Do you know how hard it is to make royal icing without regular sugar or milk? And I've got quinoa pancakes and agave syrup and chicken sausage from that special organic free-range farm down on the shore…"

Yep. I wanted to stab that nasty woman through her nasty heart. I enjoyed baking, and people seemed to really like what came out of my kitchen, but Paula was a culinary artist. Where my cakes might be a little uneven, a few of my scones with more currants than others, Paula was exact. Everything she made was absolutely perfect. If I counted the blueberries in her muffins, I had no doubt there would be the exact same number in each. That attention to detail, that driving need to get everything exactly right, was why I was sure this cookie I was about to put in my mouth would be divine.

It was. Buttery, even though I was sure there wasn't a hint of dairy in it. Crumbly without being dry. Bursting with the flavor of real toasted almonds instead of the astringent artificial-flavor taste of the grocery store cookies.

"This is really good," I muttered with my mouth full. "I can't even tell it's not real flour. Or real butter."

The tears retreated and Paula gave me a wobbly smile. "So they're not bad? *She* said they were horrible, that they were absolutely inedible."

I doubted that anything Paula made was even remotely inedible. "No, they're awesome. Keep this recipe."

She sighed. "Good. I was beginning to doubt my skills, Kay. I don't know how you're managing to make your icebox cake with all the dietary restrictions this woman has."

I shoved the rest of the cookie in my mouth and grabbed another off the plate. "I'm not. That recipe has enough butter and sugar to drop Luanne Trainor dead on the spot. The guests can eat it. I already told Nancy to make sure Luanne knows it's not in line with her dietary needs."

Paula wrinkled her nose. "She'll complain. Loudly. I get the feeling she thinks everyone else should deny themselves flour and dairy and sugar because she can't have them. It's funny because she clearly doesn't have any problem with alcohol. Downed half that bottle of the port we put in the guest rooms."

Guess the woman had to have some vices, although being

a nasty piece of work was more than enough of a vice for anyone.

"I'll leave you to the cooking and wait in the other room," I told Paula. "She's got to get out of bed soon or she'll be late to her own brunch."

I headed into the living room with the quickly cooling drinks and sat Luanne's on the end table. Should I go wake her? That really shouldn't be my job and I didn't relish the idea of seeing Luanne in bed or catching her half-naked, but perhaps she'd overslept her alarm. I'd just picked up the tea and was about to head up the stairs when a woman breezed through the front door of the B&B. She was tall and lean. Dark hair was piled up on her head in a messy bun of thick curls. She had on a black pencil skirt and a figure-hugging, lightweight, sleeveless turtleneck. Her makeup was cover-model worthy. In one hand she held a go-cup. The other was wrapped around a tablet. A huge leather bag slung over her shoulder, held tight to her waist with her elbow.

"Is she up yet?" the woman asked, her voice breathless and edging toward irritated. She glanced up the stairs as if she were an ill-prepared knight about to embark on a hopeless quest.

"Luanne? No, she's not. At least not that I can tell. I was just about to go up and brave the dragon's den." I advanced with my hand outstretched. "I'm Kay Carrera."

"Eva Zinovi." The woman stuffed the tablet in her bag and shook my hand with a firm grip. "And dragon's den is about right. Hope you brought a sword."

Zinovi. I searched my memory and recalled that Nancy had told me that was the agent's name. I'd never been so relieved. It seems the cavalry had arrived to save me from the dragon.

"I was hoping *you* brought the sword." I pushed the drink cup into her hand. "Hopefully an offering will do the job instead. Green tea. Organic free trade stuff with a splash of almond milk."

Eva looked at the name on the cup and grimaced. "She'll complain it's not from her usual shop, but she'll drink it. I'm going up. Call the police if I'm not back in ten minutes. Actually, call the coroner if I'm not back in ten minutes."

I chuckled and watched her ascend the stairs, wondering how she managed to keep her humor in the face of such a difficult client. I'm sure the paycheck helped. From what I'd read, an agency got fifteen percent of their client's earnings. When it came to Luanne Trainor, that had to be quite a chunk of change. Add in the probably true rumors of a film deal and Eva would have ample reason to put up with the author's bristly personality.

I sat back down to my coffee, grimacing as I heard thumps and raised voices from upstairs. An hour later, the enticing aroma of sausage and ham lured me into the kitchen where I eyed the breakfast preparations and swiped the plate of almond cookies to take back into the living room with me. I'd just pulled the second book in the Fanged Darkness series from my bag and was settling in for some cookies and a read when Eva came down the stairs.

"Well, she's up at least." The woman rolled her eyes. "I hate to bother our hostess, but do you think she has any coffee? For me, of course. Luanne won't touch the stuff."

I pointed to a carafe on top of a tall hunt table and watched as the agent refilled her go-cup, pouring a generous helping of whole cream in and giving it all a stir.

"Think there's anything I can grab from the kitchen to take up to her?" Eva looked at the ceiling. "She's complaining that dinner last night was inedible and that they tried to appease her with stale, cardboard cookies."

"I think Paula has some fruit cut up." I hesitated for a

second, then held out the plate. "Here. Have one of the stale, cardboard cookies."

"Fruit might do. Can't imagine what she'd find to complain about cantaloupe and strawberries, although I'm sure she'll think of something." Eva took a bite of the cookie and stared down at it with raised brows. "Wow. This is really good."

"I know. Paula is working her butt off in there for this brunch. She's gone out of her way to meet Luanne's dietary requirements, even having special flours overnighted in for these cookies. Is there anything you can do? The poor woman was in tears this morning from how mean and ungrateful Luanne has been to her."

Eva sighed. "I'll talk to her. She's always been a bit difficult, but this isn't really like her to be so horrible with fans and the general public. It's this film deal. And there were some other things in the last few months that have really stressed her out."

"That's no excuse for being mean to someone who has gone out of their way to please you. And these cookies? Come on, there's no way anyone should be complaining about these cookies!"

The agent shook her head. "Be grateful you only have to deal with her for a few days. I get this twenty-four-seven." She straightened her shoulders and shot me a bracing smile. "But that's why I make the big bucks, right? Put up with the diva and broker the deals."

I led Eva into the kitchen where she apologized profusely to Paula, being so gracious and charming that the other woman was actually smiling by the time we left with the plate of fruit.

"I'll go hurry her along," the agent told me. "Is there anything else I need to wrangle her into doing before the brunch guests get here?"

"Can you swap her out with a nicer, more pleasant doppelgänger?" I asked. "The only worry on my mind right now is that she'll be horrible either to or in front of the guests. They paid a lot of money for this."

Eva set her jaw and glared up the stairway. "I'll do what I can. This isn't really her thing, you know. She never agrees to small-venue appearances like this. I was shocked out of my mind when she told me we were coming here. Especially with everything that's going on right now. The timing is so...problematic."

I looked at her in surprise. "I thought the publisher scheduled this. Milford isn't exactly a metropolis. We were shocked as well, and it all was very last minute. I figured something big canceled and the publisher was just looking to fill a slot."

"No, this was all her idea." Eva looked up the stairs. "Her really bad idea. But it's done. My job now is to make sure she gets through the next two days without alienating half her fan base."

"Good luck with that," I muttered as I watched the agent climb the stairs. Then, grateful to leave Luanne Trainor in her hands, I sat down to finish off the cookies and read. Nancy arrived twenty minutes early to put out the place cards and the gift baskets. A few minutes before noon, the guests began to arrive.

Tonight's presentation would be held in the theater a few blocks away and those tickets had sold to over three hundred guests. The meet-and-greet was a VIP option for the first one hundred who registered, but this brunch was far pricier. Eleven people had paid big for the privilege of sitting down at a table with Luanne Trainor to share a meal and ask her whatever questions came to mind. Nancy had coordinated via e-mail with Eva to put together some general questions to get things started, and to help direct the flow of conversation, but the brunch was supposed to be pretty informal and would be a bit of a free-for-all.

I couldn't believe that Luanne had agreed to this sort of thing. She didn't strike me as the sort of person who enjoyed something so unstructured, and the ride from the airport had shown me she didn't have much in the way of small-talk or informal conversation skills. I was more nervous than Nancy, foreseeing an absolute disaster and eleven upset fans who would either want their money back or be burning their library of Luanne Trainor books after the event. Most likely both.

Unsurprisingly, the attendees were eleven women. I had no doubt that Luanne had male readers, but the ones who'd ponied up for this brunch were all women—and they were of all ages. Three seemed to be about my age or slightly older. Three looked like they'd just come from dropping their kids off at soccer practice. One seemed as if she were about to give birth before the sun set. Three were so young that I wondered if their parents knew they were reading these novels, and one sported a burping cloth over one shoulder. I motioned to it, and she yanked it off with an embarrassed wince, shoving it into a purse that looked big enough to carry a small vehicle. Every guest had at least one book clasped tightly in their hands, no doubt for an autograph.

Nancy milled about the crowd, greeting everyone while I went up to check on Luanne. Eva was there, holding the plate of fruit in one hand and a bottle of what looked to be expensive water in the other. Luanne had foregone the animal-print leggings today and had on a bright red leather miniskirt and a striped tank top that barely contained her bosom. Her shoes were not the red ones from yesterday, but were equally tall, and equally pointy as those ones. As I walked in, a blast of hairspray nearly shellacked my face.

"That's enough, Luanne. You're single-handedly

destroying the ozone layer." Eva looked over at me and rolled her eyes. I grimaced in sympathy.

"Are we ready? The guests are all here," I told them.

"It's not noon yet," Luanne snapped. "And I need another coat of mascara."

"You *need* to get your butt downstairs and start schmoozing," Eva countered. "Food's on the table at noon. I want you working the room a bit beforehand. Come on. Your eyelashes are perfect. And your hair is gravity-defying. Let's go."

I bit back a smile, very grateful that the agent had shown up to act as a buffer between me and the author. I wouldn't have had the gall to talk to her the way her long-time business associate did, and I doubt I would have been anywhere near as effective.

"Fine," Luanne snapped, grabbing the bottle of water from Eva's hands. "I hope that cow who owns this place has something decent for breakfast. Those cookies were horrible."

A cold, hard glint came into Eva's eyes. "You will eat what's on your plate and compliment her, do you hear me? This isn't the nineteenth century. Being a bit eccentric is one thing, but insulting your fans and hostess crosses the line. One social media post goes viral and you can kiss that film deal goodbye. *And* that contract offer on a third series."

Luanne snarled and threw the bottle of water across the room, where it bounced off a wall and onto the bed. "The producers don't care, and neither does the publisher. Any publicity is good publicity. I'd probably just sell more books if something like that went viral."

"Bullying your hostess to tears? The hostess who has been practicing recipes for a week to accommodate your health concerns? The hostess who overnighted in special flour to make cookies from scratch for you? Cookies that were incredible tasting? Cookies that you told her were stale and like cardboard? Luanne, you made that nice, plump, granny woman cry. That's not the kind of publicity you want. Now get your act together, get control of your mouth, and be nice for once in your damned life!"

I stared wide-eyed at the two, feeling like a complete eavesdropper, but far too nosy to scoot away. Holy moley, there was clearly a line not to cross with the tolerant, easy-going Eva Zinovi. Luanne jerked as though the other woman had hit her, her eyes narrowing as the pair commenced an epic stare-down. Finally, the author turned with a huff, pushing past me and tottering down the stairs in her high heels.

"I better go make sure she doesn't alienate the whole room," Eva muttered. "Sorry you had to see that."

"Everyone has their breaking point," I told her. "What can I do to help? Run interference with the questions? Buffer between her and Paula?"

"She'll apologize to that woman before she leaves in the morning," Eva told me with that glint back in her eyes. "Some assistance with the questions would be appreciated, though. Have you read all her books?"

"No," I confessed. "Just the first Fanged Darkness and a few chapters of book two. I started Broken Wolf and Witches Gone Wild last night, but..." Ugh, how do I tell this agent that her client's first two series were absolutely dreadful?

Turns out I didn't have to.

"What? Where the heck did you find those? They're buried so far in the product listings that they're halfway to China. The publishing company won't sell her the rights back because they're worth more on the balance sheet than the reversion fees. I was hoping they'd died a slow death and were in some unmarked grave."

"Luanne mentioned them when I was driving her back

from the airport, so I thought I'd check them out." I paused a second, searching for the right words that wouldn't come across as horribly insulting. "Lots of literary fiction isn't all that successful in terms of sales, but are wonderful works of art. I'd thought..."

"Well, you'd thought wrong." Eva laughed. "They sold okay, don't get me wrong, but that was in the early days of e-books when there wasn't a lot out there. They just don't hold up with the competition now. They're really not that well written—not anywhere nearly as good as her current stuff. I've got no idea why she's so attached to those things. I've advised her for years to just let them go and focus on the money makers."

"She's lucky," I told Eva. "Lots of authors never come around. It's like she had an epiphany or something ten years ago. Whatever happened, I'm glad. I'm totally hooked and plan on binge-reading Fanged Darkness and Infernal Awakenings through the rest of the summer."

Her dark eyes squinted up with her smile. "Good. We can always use more fans. And as for the questions, try to keep things away from Barton Wells. Other than that, Luanne should be able to field just about anything without wigging completely out."

I blinked in surprise, remembering the conversation from the airport. "What's up with Barton Wells?"

"Ever since she killed him off in book six, she's been getting hate mail. It seems he had quite the group of admirers, including several fanfiction books where they got together. It's a sore subject with her."

My jaw dropped. "Barton Wells is dead? Dead?" I felt like someone had punched me in the gut at the news, as if someone I actually knew had died.

Eva clapped a hand over her mouth. "Oh, I'm so sorry! I

forgot you haven't read that far in the series. Forget I said that. Spoilers."

"Why?" I choked out. "What happened?"

She eyed me warily. "Are you sure you want me to tell you? Spoilers, you know."

"You can't just tell me a character I loved, one I loved far more than Roman, sexy though he may be, died, and not let me know the details."

"Ah, you're one of those readers." She wiggled her eyebrows. "Like I said, there are a bunch of Barton fans. They write fanfiction about Barton and Trelanie having a happy-ever-after, and him staking Roman and all that. I told Luanne that killing him off was a bad idea, but she insisted. We got death threats. Someone mailed a cow heart to her in a box. It was a bad few months. We're still getting hate mail over that one and it was last year when that book came out."

"What happened?" I insisted.

She sighed. "Barton and Trelanie had a moment. Roman found out. End of the day, Roman didn't lift a pinky to help Barton when the ghouls swamped the condos, and he was killed. It opened a huge rift between Roman and Trelanie that lead to the events in book seven which is coming out next week. That's why everyone is wringing their hands over whether Roman and Trelanie are going to get back together again or not."

"I'm more interested in whether Barton is going to come back from the dead and kick some vampire butt," I retorted. "With or without his wheelchair."

Eva lifted both hands. "I know. I know. Just don't go mailing us any cow hearts or anything."

We made our way downstairs where Luanne was thankfully chatting politely with the attendees. Everyone clustered around her as she told a tale of her inspiration coming in a bolt of awareness while sitting on a mountaintop somewhere. She'd thought to herself: what if a strong, confident woman could turn a creature of darkness into one of light and reform a heartless, cruel vampire with the strength of her love?

It was a common trope, from Beauty and the Beast to the millions of bad-boy romance novels on the shelves, but what made this old theme new and shiny had been Luanne's writing. And no matter how much I disliked the woman, she could write a heck of a novel. At least, in the last ten years she could write a heck of a novel.

"So you didn't just remake Wicked Night, then?" the woman with the burping cloth asked.

There was a sudden chill in the room. I heard Eva suck in a breath and realized that Barton Wells wasn't the only sensitive topic as far as Luanne Trainor was concerned.

To give the woman credit, she didn't bite anyone's head off at the question. Her smile grew a little stiff, but she wasn't rude, and she did answer the question.

"I never copied off Wicked Night. I've never even read the series. There are common themes between all vampire romance novels, but I can promise you that I have never plagiarized or stolen someone else's idea. Any similarities between Star Swift's series and mine are completely coincidental."

Eva let out a breath and muttered, "Good. Just what the lawyer told her to say. We might get through this morning without a tantrum after all."

"That's what I thought," one of the soccer moms announced. "Trelanie is nothing like Belinda. And Roman is *way* sexier and brooding than Eduardo."

The rest of the attendees all chimed in their agreement on how Roman set the standard for smoking-hot vampire heroes, and in an epic battle between the two, he'd beat Eduardo to a pulp.

"I wish Barton hadn't died," one of the teen girls commented.

"Oh, I know. He was a very nice man. So polite. So considerate." One of the older women shook her head. "I'd hoped he'd find a nice young woman of his own. Not Trelanie, of course, but maybe that librarian woman."

"Why not Trelanie?" burping-cloth woman asked. "I was so thrilled to see a positive portrayal of a disabled person in a novel but shuffling him off on the librarian is wrong. There needs to be a world where a beautiful, knife-wielding woman can fall in love with a smart, capable man regardless of whether he can walk or not."

A teen with blue hair and a nose piercing snorted. "Seriously? You've got two guys to choose from and you're going to pick stuffy old Barton over the vampire who rocks the bedsheets? Who can rip through a hoard of ghouls with his bare hands? Who craves your blood like it's the very water of life?"

Ew on the blood thing, but as much as I liked Barton and felt he was the better long-term choice for a relationship, she did have a point.

"Barton rocks the bedsheets too," burping-cloth woman countered. "And at least he's not sneaking into her room at night like some deranged serial killer, or lying to her about the staff of power, or offering to share her with his Maker to get the vial with the oil of Anubis."

I was so confused. But in spite of that, and in spite of the fact that the spoilers were flying around the room, I was fascinated. It was incredible to see a group of people passionate about fictional characters, discussing their lives and their motivations as if they were real. As the woman who'd spent most of her childhood with her nose in a book, as the woman who'd majored in journalism, I wholeheartedly approved. We weren't debating Faulkner or James Joyce, but reading was reading.

"He wouldn't have *really* shared Trelanie with his Maker," one of the soccer moms protested. "That was all a ruse to get the vial. Besides, Trelanie would have kicked the Maker's butt."

"Are you kidding?" blue-hair's friend, who had normal-colored brown hair but twice the nose piercings, countered. "The Maker is three thousand years old. Trelanie never would have beaten him. And I agree. Roman is kind of a dick sometimes. Maybe Trelanie can just sleep with him every now and then but marry Barton."

Yikes. I don't know many men who would have been on board with that sort of arrangement. I thought of Eli, of my father, of my boss J.T., and Judge Beck and realized that I didn't know *any* men who would have been on board with that sort of thing.

"Barton is clearly the better man," burping-cloth woman agreed.

"Well, too bad, because Barton is dead," Luanne snapped. "Dead. Torn apart by a hoard of ghouls. So forget about him."

"Roman let those ghouls in and purposely didn't help Barton," nose-piercings girl said. "It was a total dick move on his part. I know he was jealous and all that, but if I was Trelanie, I'd never forgive him for that. Well, maybe I'd still sleep with him now and then, but I'd never forgive him."

"Did the ghouls really kill him?" pregnant woman asked. "They just found some blood and stuff. Maybe the ghouls took him away and have him captive somewhere to use as leverage. Maybe he'll enthrall them and be back with an army of ghouls to get his revenge and run off with Trelanie in his arms…in the wheelchair."

"He's dead," Luanne snarled. "Dead. What part of dead don't you understand?"

"Ooh," burping-cloth woman's eyes shot wide. "The oil of Anubis! Trelanie is furious with Roman, right? So she goes and sleeps with the Maker and he gives her the vial—"

"Because Trelanie is such a good lay that the Maker is gonna give up the oil of Anubis for one night?" the other teen girl without any piercings at all countered. "I mean, I'd do a lot for some quality naked time with Trelanie, but I wouldn't be giving up something like that just for a quickie in the sack. No, she's going to have to give up her soul or something."

"Barton would be devastated," pregnant woman told her. "Trelanie giving up her soul to bring him back from the dead? That's a bargain he never would have wanted her to make."

"Dead!" Luanne shouted. Everyone ignored her.

"But then Roman can fight the Maker," burping-cloth woman added enthusiastically. "Trelanie losing her soul pushes him over the edge and gives him the strength to face the Maker and kill him, which would give Trelanie her soul back."

"But Roman should be mortally wounded in the fight," one of the older women said. "And he dies in Trelanie's arms. Then she and Barton ride off into the sunset…on his wheelchair."

"Dead!" Luanne screamed, her voice reaching the pitch of a harpy. "I'm the author. I get to say what happens to these people and Barton does not get Trelanie. He's just some side character. He's not sexy. He's boring and he's in a wheelchair. And he's dead. The ghouls killed him. He's dead and he's not coming back!"

Everyone stared at her. And as if on cue, Paula poked her head in the door, a cheerful if somewhat nervous smile on her face as she announced that breakfast was ready.

I had no doubt brunch would be delicious…and awkward.

CHAPTER 7

By the time I got home, I was wishing I could fast-forward through the rest of the weekend and shove Luanne Trainor on a plane. Brunch had been awkward, as expected, although Luanne had recovered her composure enough to thank Paula for the wonderful food and insist that the woman give her the quinoa pancake recipe. Our hostess's tears had evaporated at the kind words, and she'd spent the rest of the brunch flitting about like an overly caffeinated butterfly.

She was the only one. The eleven guests asked their carefully worded questions about how many books would be in the series, if there would be a third series featuring Morgana, and if Luanne had any intentions of revisiting the characters from Infernal Awakenings in the future. Questions about the much-rumored film deal were coyly turned aside by Eva, to be addressed at the actual presentation later that day.

Things had lightened up a bit as the plates were cleared. The books were signed, and Eva had led a spirited discussion on which actors and actresses should play Roman and Trelanie if the rumors of a film deal were true. No further mention was made of Barton and his sad fate. Still, I was glad to head home, well aware that I'd be turning around and driving back in another few hours.

Taco greeted me with a meow at the door, purring loudly as he serpentined around my legs. I picked him up, reminding him that I'd fed him earlier that morning. He butted his head against my cheek, so warm and affectionate in my arms that I had no choice but to head for the kitchen and the bag of cat treats I'd hidden in the cabinet next to the flour.

"Don't tell anyone, okay?" I asked as he chirruped and eagerly took the treat from my fingers.

"Don't tell anyone what? That you're slipping treats to your fat cat? The one you keep putting on a diet?"

I smiled up at Judge Beck. "These are low-calorie cat treats. Any nutritionist will tell you that a diet is doomed to failure if you deny yourself anything pleasurable at all. I'm just ensuring Taco's long-term weight-loss success by allowing him the occasional healthy snack."

One of Judge Beck's eyebrows shot up. "Bacon cheese Kitty Nibblers are a healthy snack? The half of a lemon cream cookie you so carelessly dropped on the floor last night is a healthy snack? And wasn't Taco licking the ground beef bowl from the meatloaves yesterday?"

"Look at this face." I turned my cat and held him up so the judge could better see him. "Can you say 'no' to this face? I can't say 'no' to this face."

He grinned, taking the cat from my arms. "Okay, but I don't want to hear you scolding any of us for allowing him the occasional 'healthy snack.' Hypocrite."

I sighed, wondering if there were such things as cat treadmills. I'd been restricting Taco's outdoor activity to the enclosed cat-run ever since I'd realized he'd been taking daily jaunts across the street to Mr. Peter's house and pestering the

Lars' dog, but he really wasn't getting as much exercise as he used to. Roaming around the house begging for food and watching the world from a six-by-eight enclosed pen wasn't the same as chasing insects, climbing trees, and trotting around an entire neighborhood. No amount of diet was going to counter his change in activity levels—especially since none of us in the household seemed to be able to resist his pleas for treats.

Should I start letting him out again? I knew it would make him happy, but I worried he'd be hit by a car crossing the road or mauled by a neighborhood dog. Although he did seem to be car-savvy, and he was pretty good about darting away once a dog decided he'd had enough sassy-cat teasing for the day.

"What do you think?" I asked the judge. "Should I start letting him outside again? I mean outside of the cat run? He's so unhappy trapped in here or in the pen, but if something ever happened to him..."

"It's your call, Kay."

I wrinkled my nose at him. "That's not helping me. Stop being a lawyer and weigh in one way or the other."

He chuckled and sat my cat down on the floor. "I know this is going to come back to bite me when I start whining about not wanting Madison to go out on a date, or Henry to go skydiving or something, but you can't wrap Taco in bubble wrap and keep him safe from life. Do everything you can to make sure he's healthy and taken care of but let him be a cat. Life is short. And cat lives are even shorter. Shouldn't he be happy chasing grasshoppers and rolling in Suzette's catnip patch, even if it means there's a risk something might happen? Heck, Kay, something might happen here. He could...choke on a chicken bone or run out of lives falling down the stairs or something."

"That does it. No more chicken unless it's boneless. And

I'm putting soft-edge bumpers on the stairs," I half-teased. But he was right. Taco loved being here with us, jumping on our laps for pets, or snoozing on the couch, but he was bored. And a lot of his begging for food probably came from that boredom.

"I just…I can't stand the thought that something might happen to him," I confessed. "I can't stand to lose anyone else I love. It's too soon to face that. If he were to not come home one night, and I were to find him by the side of the road…" My voice choked on the words.

"I know, Kay," the judge said softly. "The kids would be devastated. Me too. I've grown pretty fond of the little fur ball."

I gave him a wobbly smile. "The not-so-little fur ball."

"It needs to be your call, Kay," he said. "Personally, I would start letting him out, maybe during the day when everyone is at work and the Lars' dog is safely inside. That's my opinion. And when I break out into a sweat about Madison dating, you can remind me I told you to let the cat be happy and let him out of the house."

"Okay. Maybe on Sunday an hour or so before I feed him dinner so he knows to come back." I turned to start pulling ingredients from the cabinets. "What's on your agenda today? Golf?"

"I golfed early." He straddled a bar stool next to the kitchen island and watched me. "I'm hoping to pull a Taco and lick the bowl of whatever you're getting ready to make there."

"Icebox cake. I made a batch yesterday, but got to thinking it might not be enough, so I'm making another. It's lick-worthy. Enough butter and sugar to put you into cardiac arrest though."

"Just the sort of dessert I like. Is this for your after-party, or whatever it is you're doing tonight? The thing you're hosting for that author woman, right?"

I started opening the butter that had been softening on the counter since yesterday. "Yes, that *thing*." Although I was putting this batch in two containers so I could leave one here for us to eat later. I frowned, thinking about tonight's event. "I'll be glad when this *thing* is over, frankly. I think Nancy will be glad when it's over as well. She may resign from the committee after this one."

He laughed. "That bad? Isn't this the woman who writes those scandalous vampire books everyone is tittering about? She's as drama-ridden as her novels, I'm guessing?"

"Worse." I plopped the first stick of butter into the bowl and unwrapped the second one. "She's not a very nice person. And she killed Barton Wells."

Judge Beck blinked a few times. "I'm assuming that's not a matter for police involvement even though it sounds like a homicide?"

"He's a character in one of her books," I explained as I unwrapped the third stick of butter. "Tell me, if you had to choose between a super-hot psychopath who you couldn't trust and who might kill you, but who was really good in bed, and a nice, smart, loyal, dependable person who was in a wheelchair but who loved you, who would you pick?"

Judge Beck suddenly had the expression of a cornered animal. "Uh, which one am I supposed to pick?"

"The nice one, of course." I threw the fourth stick of butter into the bowl with unnecessary violence. "Because Barton Wells doesn't sneak in your bedroom window at night and hover over you, watching like some creepy serial killer."

"Probably because he's in a wheelchair and the window is six feet off the ground?" Judge Beck held up his hands at my glare. "Sorry, sorry. I'm picking the nice one before I get a spatula upside the head."

"I get that he's not the hero, that the sexy psychopath vampire is going to end up with the girl, but she didn't have to go and kill him," I argued, dumping half a bag of sugar into a glass measuring cup.

"Wait, the heroine killed this Barton guy? Because that pretty much gives you her decision right there."

"No! Trelanie didn't kill Barton, the ghouls did. Roman let them in and didn't help Barton and he died. I meant Luanne Trainor killed him. She's the author. She killed him. She could have sent him to Siberia or given him a love interest of his own or something. She didn't have to go and kill him."

Judge Beck rubbed his hands over his face. "This is probably going to get me banished to the garage for the night, but here goes. I'd pick the sexy psychopath, because I'm a guy and she's super-hot and that's hard to resist. But it wouldn't last because the first time she snuck through my bedroom window and stared at me sleeping, or hacked my cell phone, or was mean to my kids, she'd be gone so fast her head would spin. In the long term, I'd end up with whoever I enjoyed spending time with the most, because at my age sex is only a few times a month if I'm lucky, and the rest of my time involves non-sex things like talking about what we should have for dinner, or when the SUV needs an oil change, or who's free to take the kids to the football game Friday night. Ultimately, I want someone I can relax with, unwind with, share my life with. And if earth-shattering sex comes along with that, then sign me up."

That was probably the rightest thing he ever could have said. He admitted to the lure of superficial attraction, but in the end knew it wouldn't be enough, that it wouldn't hold without all the other things that make a relationship work. I'd been attracted to Eli from day one, but in the end, it had been all the other things that held our relationship together. Actually, in the end after his accident, it had been the memories, the reminders of the other things, that held our relationship together. That and our vows. *In sickness and in health. Till death do us part...*

"After Eli's accident..." I trailed off, my face suddenly hot. What was I doing? I couldn't confess to this good-looking roommate of mine that I hadn't had earth-shattering sex in ten years. That I hadn't had sex at all in ten years.

His eyes softened. "Barton Wells. I'd take Barton Wells in a heartbeat. Well, the female version of Barton Wells, anyway."

Time to lighten this conversation up a bit. "But maybe a night or two with the female version of Roman, just to cross it off your bucket list?"

"Crossing that 'hot sex with a vampire' item off a bucket list isn't an opportunity anyone should pass up," he teased.

"Maybe you'll luck out and find a weird combo of Barton and Roman?" I asked. "I'll have to suggest that to Luanne Trainor, because as I've learned this morning, she's so open to fan suggestions about what she should do regarding her characters."

"Ah, sarcasm. I know sarcasm when I hear it." He grinned. "I take it that this was a topic of discussion during what should have been a relaxing brunch with a famous author?"

I set the mixer to creaming the butter and sugar then turned to the judge. "First, she brought Paula to tears by insulting the amazing gluten- and dairy-free cookies she'd been working weeks to perfect, then she went all diva up in her bedroom with her saint of an agent minutes before the brunch. *Then,* she blows a gasket because the attendees were having a lively debate over the Barton versus Roman issue and if Barton would possibly be resurrected in the future."

He winced. "Sounds like she needs to develop some thicker skin."

"Totally. She tried to turn it around by being all nice and gracious during the actual brunch, but when you've screamed at eleven people who paid big bucks to meet you in a private setting, it's kinda hard to recover."

"And that's your attempt to sweeten them up?" He nodded at the butter and sugar mixture.

"Icebox cake sweetens everyone up." I had no idea how old the recipe was. It had been in my family as far back as 1920—possibly even earlier. It was basically the most decadent buttercream icing ever in vanilla and chocolate, separated by layers of ladyfingers. There was nothing richer, more fattening, or more delicious in the entire universe.

"Do I get some?" Judge Beck eyed the mixer.

"Are you going to the meet-and--greet?"

He grimaced. "I seriously have to sit through hundreds of women gushing about some fictional vampire in order to get a few bites of that?"

I wanted to string him along a bit, but I was too nice to let the poor guy suffer. "I'll set aside a little bit for you before I put it together. I expect you to grovel at my feet later though, and maybe peel me some grapes. Icebox cake is a special thing in my family."

"If it's as good as you say, I'll absolutely grovel at your feet. You can peel your own grapes, though."

I waved a spatula at him. "Deal."

CHAPTER 8

I hauled my cooler with the double batch of ice box cake through the lobby and stuck it in the office of the theater. There were refrigerators behind the bar area, but I didn't fully trust that someone wouldn't decide to partake early. Such was the seductive lure of icebox cake.

As I was heading out of the office I heard voices down by the dressing rooms and went to investigate, wondering if a miracle had occurred and Luanne had actually arrived to the theater early and on her own accord.

As I got closer, I realized that one of the voices was Eva, and the other was a man's voice—not Luanne's. I hesitated, then because I'm nosy, I crept closer. His voice was low and muffled, but he sounded stern, as if he were conveying something that was urgently important.

Eva was breathless and anxious. "I had no idea," she told him. "I swear neither the publisher nor I knew. We'll fix this. I promise we'll fix this."

"You better." Those words of his were very clear. "If not, then the deal's off. And if the deal's off, *my* head is the one on the chopping block."

I heard footsteps and I walked forward, rounding the corner and smiling as I passed a scowling man in a dark gray suit.

"Is Luanne here?" I asked Eva.

She blinked at me, then shook her head. "No, she's still at the inn. Can you go get her? There's no way she can walk in those heels and I've got a few quick things I need to do here first."

"Sure. I'll just check in on Nancy, then walk down to the inn. I've already arranged for Gene to give her a ride up if you didn't." I hesitated then reached out to pat the woman's shoulder. "It'll all be okay. We'll just get through tonight, then we can all breathe easy."

"If only," she muttered, then she gave me a forced smile and turned to go into the dressing room.

I found Nancy up front, organizing the volunteers who would act as ushers guiding people to their seats, as well as the ticket scanners, and the two people tending the bar and refreshment area. The contracted lighting and sound people were already setting up, and Nancy assured me that she had this end of the event well in hand, so I trotted the three blocks up to the B&B to gather our guest speaker.

Paula's husband, Gene, met me at the door of the inn, looking as if he'd aged ten years in the last twenty-four hours.

"Please tell me that woman is leaving tonight," he begged.

"Tomorrow morning," I told him. "Nine sharp. I promise I'll show up promptly and haul her to the airport and out of your hair. Hang in there until then."

"I can't take much more of her complaints. And Paula is in tears again because that woman demanded some cauliflower bread avocado and vegan cheese sandwiches and she doesn't have any recipes for that kind of stuff. Who the heck makes bread out of cauliflower anyway? Stuff gives you gas and tastes like an old gym sock."

"Well, Eva sent me to collect her. Can you bring your car around to the front?" I asked.

"Will do. I'm not surprised that agent woman sent you. They had a huge fight a few hours ago and she stormed out."

Great. Lovely. Now I would have to summon every last bit of diplomacy and deal with an angry Luanne. Well, angrier than usual, anyway. I headed up the stairs, chanting to myself that I only had to put up with her for another sixteen hours, give or take, then I could open a bottle of wine and congratulate myself for having survived the ordeal.

I knocked and entered at Luanne's terse command to find her apparently ready to go, sitting on the edge of the bed with her purse over her shoulder and a leather briefcase in one hand. As much as I disliked her, I felt a twinge of sympathy because she looked so very despondent.

"Everything okay?" I asked, not sure I wanted to know the answer.

She jerked around in surprise at my words. "Oh! I thought you were Eva. Is she downstairs?"

"She's at the theater." I eyed her closely. "Are you ready? Normally we'd just walk, but I remembered what you said about your shoes yesterday, so I arranged for Gene to give us a lift and drop us off out front."

She looked down at the sky-high cream patent-leather platform pumps on her feet and nodded. "Guess we better go then."

"Yep. Guess we better." She still didn't rise from the bed, so I stood there, not sure what to do.

With a sigh, she stood then gave me a sideways smile that was the closest thing to engaging that she'd been since I met her. "Kay, ever feel like karma is catching up to you like a freight train coming down the tracks?"

No, because I tried to live my life in such a way that there wouldn't be a bucket-load of bad karma hanging over my head. But I could hardly tell her that and not sound preachy and judgmental.

"Are you worried about the question and answer session?" I asked. "We can try to deflect any questions about Barton Wells, but since it's impromptu, I can't guarantee it won't come up."

She laughed and it sounded tinny and hollow. "That was a stupid move on my part. How the heck was I to know there was a group of fans in love with the guy? He was a sidekick. I'd intended him to die from book one. And I hate to cave to pressure and bring him back at this point. What kind of author would I be to do that? What sort of artistic integrity would I have?"

"They're your characters, your story," I told her. "But the problem with a long series like this, with well-written books that have characters who resonate with readers, is people develop their own fantasies, their own stories about them. They take hold of these characters and want them to go on journeys that are different from what you intended. It's not right or wrong, it just is." I shrugged. "But to be honest, I liked Barton a lot and am not thrilled that he got killed off."

"If that was the only thing I'd done wrong in my career, I'd be happy." She gathered up her purse and briefcase and took a few steps forward. "Let's get this over with. Hopefully this guy's car is reasonably clean and doesn't smell like old French fries and body odor."

And just like that, I hated her again.

We arrived just as the early birds were beginning to file through the door and needed to pause for several photo ops and book signings. I finally managed to whisk Luanne away and around to the back, showing her the dressing room that had been prepped for her, complete with a vase of flowers and a platter of fruit. Leaving her there, I roamed the backstage area, hoping to find Eva and do some sort of hand-off of responsibility. I'd gotten the woman here, now it was someone else's turn to make sure she got onto the stage at the correct time while I helped with the arriving guests. It took me a while to locate Nancy in what had become a thick crowd of women, but finally I managed to spot her out by the entrance.

"Have you seen Eva?" I asked, shooting an apologetic glance at the woman she'd been talking with. "Luanne is in the dressing room, but I don't trust her to get on stage in time without someone urging her along."

"Back in the alleyway having a smoke," Nancy told me. "And the caterers are set to bring in tables a few minutes after eight."

"Thanks." It would be a quick changeover. The speaking event ended at eight and we somehow needed to get everyone who hadn't registered for the meet-and-greet out the door through the very same room where we'd be trying to set up tables of food. Maybe we could usher people out the side door into the walkway alley, although it didn't seem that polite or feasible to shove nearly three hundred women into a narrow passageway between two buildings like cattle through a chute.

I headed that way, and did indeed find Eva in the alleyway, her back against the neighboring building's fire door as she smoked a cigarette. I was a bit surprised. Did anyone smoke cigarettes anymore? All the kids seemed to be vaping nowadays, and pretty much all the people my age and up had quit aside from a few holdouts.

"Hey." She shot me a tired smile and stubbed the smoke out against the side of the fire door. "Nasty habit. I had to bum one off the sound guy. It's been two years since I've needed one of these."

"That bad?" I asked. "I would have thought you'd be used to her tantrums by now." Although maybe it wasn't just Luanne that had her on edge. Things had seemed pretty tense between her and that man she'd been talking with earlier.

"Luanne screwed up. Bad. I'm not sure how we're going to fix it and the timing is…" She grimaced. "Problematic."

Huh. Maybe that was what the earlier conversation had been about. I felt for the agent, really, I did, but we had over three hundred guests coming to hear this author speak, then a hundred staying afterward. Unless the screw up involved those two events, it had to take a definite back seat.

"Well, Luanne is in her dressing room getting ready. And if it's any consolation, she seems unusually subdued right now. Whatever you both fought about, I think she's sorry."

Eva sighed and pushed away from the fire door. "Yeah, well, sorry doesn't cut it anymore. Over ten years together and the woman's become something of a friend to me. Well, not really a friend. More like a frenemy. But either way, as a professional client, she sucks. There are times I'd like to take a frying pan to the side of her head."

Suddenly I was everyone's confessor. And normally my gossipy self would love that, but I had an event to get going here. Nancy was counting on my help.

"Lights flash ten before the hour getting everyone into their seats," I told Eva. "We need Luanne on stage directly after, and we'll present her right after the announcements."

"We'll be there. With bells on." Eva shot me a wry glance as she headed into the theater. I went in after her and shoved the brick aside that smokers used to prop the door open when they were taking a break, shutting the fire door tight.

True to her word, Eva had Luanne seated on stage right after the lights flashed. The agent sat to one side of the author, and on the other was the guy who had been talking to the agent. He was a beefy middle-aged man. The lights reflected off his bald head, and his tailored suit strained against his folded arms. I had no idea who this guy was or why he was on stage with the others, but he didn't look any happier now then he had earlier.

The audience applause was thunderous as Nancy introduced Luanne. The woman had shed her earlier malaise and had miraculously transformed from the diva she'd been the last few days into a smiling, animated celebrity. She introduced Eva, gushing her thanks for the woman's invaluable assistance in guiding her career and both negotiating and closing her various contracts. Then Luanne turned with a smile to the man, stating that she had a big surprise for the audience, and would be introducing him later.

Was I the only one who saw how stiff and wooden that smile was?

Knowing the behind-the-scenes tension didn't negate the fact that Luanne Trainor's presentation was mesmerizing. She told of her inspiration for the Infernal Awakenings series, and how the success of those novels led her to explore the idea of taking a minor character—Trelanie——and developing a series based on her and featuring vampires as opposed to demons. She talked about the push-and-pull of a slow-burn, although intensely erotic, romance and how she maintained the sexual tension between Trelanie and Roman throughout the series. At the end, everyone was all starstruck, even me, and I had seen the woman at what was surely her worst.

Whatever Luanne Trainor might be in person, up on stage she was just as much an entertainer as she was on the page.

The author took a break at this point in her narrative and said that before getting to the evening's exciting announcements, she wanted to field questions from the audience. With a wave of her finger, she warned us she'd not be revealing anything that would spoil upcoming books but was happy to discuss anything about the current novels, the characters, or general worldbuilding.

There were a few excited questions about the nature of Trelanie's magic weapon, and if Roman immediately burned to ash in the sunlight or was there some wiggle room as far as exposure time, and if it were possible, magically or otherwise, for the two to have babies.

Half-vampire babies? I guess anything was possible in the world of fiction.

Then a woman stood in the back of the room patiently awaiting the microphone, her perfectly coiffed hair sprayed into a helmet of gold surrounding her lean face. As the volunteer with the mic approached, my eyes turned to her. I heard a soft gasp from the stage and could practically feel the tension.

Unfortunately, the volunteer with the mic didn't feel the tension and hopped right up to the woman, handing the device over.

"Yes, my question is how do you sleep at night knowing you've plagiarized every single thing you've written?'"

The audience froze then turned slowly to stare at the woman. I, on the other hand, stared at Luanne Trainor. The author went white, then red, then looked like a puffer fish about ready to blow.

Eva got to her feet and took the microphone from Luanne, calm and cool as ice in a glass of lemonade. "That lawsuit was dismissed, Ms. Swift. The plagiarism charges you brought against Ms. Trainor were without merit. And this is hardly the place to discuss your wild accusations."

Swift. Star Swift. I remembered that Eva had mentioned the lawsuit about how Luanne's Fanged Darkness series was plagiarized from Ms. Swift's Wicked Night series. A stressful year indeed. This lawsuit, the fan furor over Barton Wells. It did explain some of Luanne's less-endearing moments, although I got the idea those were more personality traits than situationally stress--induced nastiness.

"The stories are identical to mine," Star Swift insisted. "She changed the names and a few of the plot details, but they're the same books."

Poor Nancy had a horrified expression on her face. She glanced over at me as if I could help out, but I didn't know what to do either. We hadn't prepared for this sort of thing. It wasn't like we had bouncers to escort the woman out, although looking back on the situation, we should have had our volunteer just take the mic and walk away. Although Star Swift might have continued, shouting to make herself heard without the mic.

Note to self: we probably needed to have bouncers next time. I doubted if the environmentalist guy from the local college would draw the kind of crowd who might require a bouncer, but just in case...

Luanne snatched the microphone back from her agent. "You can't copyright ideas, Star. There's a million vampire romances out there. You don't see Mary Shelley suing me now, do you?"

I winced. Mary Shelley, who was long dead, wrote Frankenstein, not erotic vampire romances. Still, I understood her point. There *were* a million vampire romances out there, all variations on a theme. Just because Luanne Trainor had a steamy series with common themes didn't mean she'd lifted her stories from another author. Those who hit the big-time tended to attract these kinds of lawsuits, and most of them *were* without merit, from desperate people who were looking for any reason one author's series had gone bestseller where theirs remained unread. But I'd been a journalist in my youth, and I'd seen my share of carefully manipulated story-theft. It might not violate copyright but mosaic plagiarism crossed some serious ethical lines in my opinion. And sadly, there were a lot of people who felt it was a perfectly acceptable way to make a living by lifting someone else's work, putting a fresh coat of paint on it, then releasing it as their own.

The two authors started to yell at each other, and I beckoned for Nancy to go get the mic. She ran up the stairs faster than I'd ever see her move and snatched it from Star Swift's hands, giving her a bad-cop worthy glare.

"Thank you. Thank you for that comment. We'll be taking some additional questions at the end of the night, and those of you who have registered for our meet-and-greet will have an opportunity to ask Luanne Trainor your questions personally."

Ugh. I hoped Star Swift hadn't bought a meet-and-greet ticket or we were going to have a problem.

Eva motioned Luanne aside and took her place, repeating Nancy's comments then saying she, as Luanne's agent, was thrilled to be announcing something everyone had been waiting to hear.

"Fanged Darkness has sold the film rights to the series, and we expect the first adaptation to hit the movie theaters in the next two years."

The audience went crazy with applause and shrieks of joy. Half the theater rose to their feet in a standing ovation. Once the excitement had calmed down, Eva turned and motioned to the man behind her. The man who was still seated. The man who continued to have a scowl on his face.

"And here from White Night Studios is assistant producer, Sebastian Codswim!"

I'd never seen someone so reluctant to walk to the podium and discuss a film deal that had the entire audience abuzz. Was it the problem he'd been discussing with Eva before the event? It couldn't be that big of a deal. Eva had said she'd take care of it, and surely she wouldn't have made the announcement if it wasn't completely a done deal?

Maybe he didn't like Luanne Trainor, or he didn't like vampire novels and movies. Perhaps he doubted that the book sales would translate into money at the box office? I didn't. I'd only read one and a half books and I would be at the movie theater on opening day. I was pretty sure a huge percentage of readers would as well. And nothing sold books like the announcement of a film deal. Luanne's books would skyrocket back up the charts again, no doubt staying for months at the top of all the lists as hordes of people picked the book up in anticipation of the movie, wanting to see what all the talk was about.

"We're excited about the licensing of film rights for the Fanged Darkness series," the man said. "And we anticipate beginning production just as soon as the appropriate signatures are obtained on the contracts to ensure legal transfer of rights. After that, the studio will be making a formal announcement. Thank you."

That had to have been the most flat, unemotional, boring speech in the history of mankind. It didn't seem to dampen audience enthusiasm, but I noticed Eva looked as though she were about to have a heart attack. The man shoved the mic back at Luanne, and the author continued to expand on her earlier topics, cautiously again opening the floor to questions.

Was I the only one who noticed Eva and the producer guy having a quiet, close, heated discussion back at their chairs? What the heck was going on? Surely he wouldn't have come all the way out here to announce the film deal if there were any issues. Unless the issues had just come up in the last twenty-four hours. Or perhaps the issues were the reason he'd come to a tiny town in the middle of nowhere.

That would explain his sour expression and peculiar statements about contracts and legalities. Who was dragging their feet about signing off on the film deal? Surely not Luanne who had probably already assigned those rights to the publishing company. And surely not the publishing company who would stand to make a ton of money on a movie and related sales and merchandise.

Unless there was another offer in the wings, and they were stalling to see if that was a better deal. But if that was the case, then why announce this at a public session and risk looking like idiots and upsetting a whole room full of fans?

It probably didn't matter. These things always got sorted out in the end. Right now, my focus was on making sure none of the other questions sparked Luanne's temper. That and meeting the caterers up front to set up for the meet-and-greet.

Get through tonight. That was my goal. Get through tonight without any further issues, then manage to get Luanne to the airport tomorrow without me or anyone else killing her.

CHAPTER 9

Daisy was scooping more icebox cake onto a plate loaded down with ham salad sandwiches and chips. It was her second helping. Suzette, Olive, and Kat stood beside her, each of them with their own plate of the decadent dessert. The first container was already gone—practically licked clean—and we were now halfway through the second batch. I smiled, smug that my contribution had been a big hit.

And so far, knock on wood, the meet-and-greet had gone smoothly. Luanne was on her best behavior, a stiff smile plastered on her face as she signed books and answered questions from fans. The producer guy had vanished once he'd realized that the main event had finished. Eva stayed, keeping a sharp eye on Luanne and doing her part to be social as well.

"Ham salad. Ham salad. More ham salad." Nancy flitted by me, calling out instructions to the catering staff.

Daisy looked up and grinned, her eyes meeting mine. "Icebox cake. Icebox cake. More icebox cake."

I laughed. "Any more and you'll be leaving here in an ambulance. That's all I've got. Pace yourself."

Daisy stuck a forkful of the dessert into her mouth. "It's totally worth a trip to the hospital, especially if the paramedics are cute."

"Did you all get your books signed?" There was quite a crowd around Luanne and I wanted to make sure my friends had a chance at autographs.

"First thing." Suzette hefted the huge tote bag she'd slung over her shoulder. "I've got everyone's books in here. Olive scored some playing cards with the book covers on the back, too. They'll make poker night extra special."

"There's a poker night?" I teased.

"There will be now," Suzette shot back. Then her eyes drifted over toward the group around the author. "Oh, look! Someone's in costume. That's so cool. I wish I had the guts to do something like that."

I turned and saw a woman with black leather pants and a camo tank top, bandoliers holding amulets and vials full of colored liquid crisscrossing her chest. Her wig of dark hair was in a long braid down her back and she'd done a great job recreating Trelanie's tattoos as well as her signature scar across her left bicep. Everyone made room for her, admiring her outfit as she shyly held a book out for Luanne.

"Impressive," the author told her, signing inside the book jacket with a flourish before handing it back. "Now go fight some ghouls and save the world."

"That's my job. I'm here to save the world." A blonde woman with fashionably retro cat-eye glasses and frayed skinny jeans pushed her way to the front of the crowd, nearly knocking the cosplay girl over as she came face-to-face with the author.

Then she pulled out a knife—a real, metal, non-plastic knife.

It was like Moses parting The Red Sea the way everyone jumped away from her. Luanne turned whiter than the marble floors. No one stepped up to defend the author or confront the woman with the knife, and I found myself again thinking that we probably needed to have a bouncer at these events. A bouncer and a metal detector.

The woman extended the knife toward Luanne, not in a stabby sort of way, but more as if she wanted the woman to take it in hand by the blade. "I'm here. I've come to protect you and escort you safely to the hinterland. Roman is outside guarding the perimeter."

Did this woman think she was the heroine of Luanne's novels? Or was she here to offer a replica knife as a gift to the author, and her boyfriend, coincidently named Roman, was a police officer or a security guard ensuring the plagiarism woman didn't come back? Either way, she had the wrong end of the knife pointed toward our guest.

"Hey, easy with that thing." Daisy stepped forward, her hands upraised. My friend, the social worker with a soft heart, the yoga guru, and the brave confronter of knife-wielding fans. "Is that Trelanie's knife you've got there? It's beautiful. The detail on the hilt is a work of art."

The woman turned slightly and Luanne edged to the side, carefully putting distance between herself and the knife.

"It kills ghouls," the woman confessed. She'd rotated the knife in her hands to show Daisy the etchings on the hilt. "They're magic runes. Spelled against the undead."

Out of the corner of my eye I saw Nancy on the phone, no doubt with the police, but my concern right now was for my friend.

"Can I see it?" Daisy smiled warmly at the woman, her tone full of respect and admiration. "I work magic myself, and I can see the aura around this knife. It's clearly the work of a talented master."

The woman hesitated, eyeing Daisy suspiciously. The thing was, my friend was partially telling the truth. I knew she did things she called magic in her Wiccan circles, but from what I'd heard, they were mostly to help someone find a desperately needed job, bring positive energy to a friend suffering from depression, or to provide strength to a coworker going through a hard time. They were like the prayer circles at my church, not etching the hilt of a dagger so it could slay undead.

Although maybe Daisy did that sort of thing, too. I saw ghosts and one of them liked to roll potatoes off my kitchen counter. If there were ghouls roaming beneath the streets of Locust Point, I was pretty sure Daisy would be the one to single-handedly stop them.

We all held a breath as the woman extended the knife, point first, toward Daisy. Luanne was almost free of the corner she was boxed into.

Daisy took a step to the side and in, so she was perpendicular to the woman, the side of the blade less than a foot from her chest. She leaned forward, making admiring murmuring noises, then held out her hands as if she were about to receive a sacrament, giving the other woman a hesitant smile. She looked up at my friend through those cat-eye glasses, then gently put the knife in her hands.

The room exploded into action, and that was when I realized that the police had arrived. One grabbed knife-woman, putting her on the floor and cuffing her as they read her Miranda rights. The other took the knife from Daisy, placing it into a bag. The whole time the woman screamed that we were all going to be eaten by ghouls unless they let her go and gave her the knife back. As the police perp-walked her out the door, she started shouting for Roman to meet her at the police station. And to bring bail money.

"Do you think there really is a Roman outside?" I asked

Daisy, putting a shaky hand on her shoulder. She'd been so close to that knife, and I'd had no idea what was running through that woman's head. What if she'd stabbed Daisy? What if she'd hurt or killed my friend?

"It might be all in her imagination. Or it might be she found a boyfriend just as unstable as she is to play the part of Roman." Daisy blew a breath out between her teeth as her shoulders slumped. "I hope one of the officers takes a look around the building, just to make sure. I'd hate for any of us to get knifed by some guy in a black cape who thought we were ghouls."

Yeah, that would just be the icing on the cake for this evening. "You were awesome, Daisy," I told her. "I can't believe you talked her into giving up her knife like that. We were all frozen. If it had been up to the rest of us, Luanne would probably have been skewered."

"From what I've heard, that wouldn't have been too much of a tragedy." Daisy grinned. "And that woman with the knife wasn't all that difficult. You work with troubled teens all day, you learn how to defuse a situation and how to disarm someone peacefully—whether it's a knife, a can of hair spray, or the metal arm off an AV projector."

"Well, you deserve a medal."

I looked around for Luanne, thinking it would be nice if the woman delivered some -much-deserved thanks in person to the one person who'd come between her and a knife. With a quick word to Daisy, I went to look for her, finding the author back in the dressing room we'd set up for her. She was in the chair, her head in her hands, her purse and briefcase on the floor beside her.

"Are you okay?" I asked, wondering for a moment where Eva was. I hadn't seen the agent in the room at all during the knife incident.

Luanne lifted her head and took a deep breath. "Yeah. You

think I'd be used to it after all the hate mail I got when I killed off Barton Wells."

"Having someone point a knife at you is a bit different than hate mail." I walked into the room and pulled a bottle of water from the box by the door, handing it to her.

"Thanks." She unscrewed the lid and downed half the contents of the bottle. "I got a heart, too."

For a second, I thought she meant that she *had* a heart, that under the detestable diva she was a good person. Then I realized she was still talking about the hate mail. "That was last year though, right? You haven't gotten any hearts in the mail recently, have you?"

She shook her head. "Doesn't matter. Angry fans, crazy knife-wielding fans, that pain-in-the-butt Star with her plagiarism accusations, and now that idiot Sebastian." She set the bottle on the dressing table and stood up, taking a few tottering steps forward on her ridiculously high heels. "Well, the show must go on and all that. One more hour for me to tap dance while Rome burns around me."

I watched her leave then went over and sniffed the contents of the water bottle, not sure whether Luanne was drunk or still reeling from the encounter with the crazy knife-woman. It smelled like water.

"One hour," I repeated to the empty room. I wasn't tap dancing, and as far as I knew, neither Rome nor anywhere else was burning, but I'd still be glad when this evening was over and I was one step closer to putting Luanne Trainor on a plane and getting back to my normal life once more.

CHAPTER 10

"Where the heck is she?" Nancy hissed. "I need her to do a photo shoot with people as they leave. Can you go track her down and put a cattle prod to her butt? Ooh, I hate dealing with these divas. Darn near gonna give me an ulcer with her ketonic no-croissant-eating diet and her run-this-here-and-that-there demands. An ulcer, Kay. An ulcer."

Luanne had emerged from the dressing room and continued her tap dance with the fans, but the event was almost over and it seemed the author had vanished again.

I patted Nancy on the shoulder. "I'll find her. She's probably just taking some time to get a drink of water. She deserves a break to compose herself after that run-in with crazy fangirl. She might be a diva, but she *did* bounce back from that pretty well. Most people would have called it a night and gone back to the inn after that happened."

"Gah, can anything else go wrong today?" Nancy made like she was pulling her hair out at the roots. "First Paula in tears over the food, then Luanne biting people's heads off over that Bert character, then the plagiarism woman, then nutsy fangirl with a knife. Please, Lord, just let me get through tonight."

"I've got it. Go have a glass of wine and some of that ham salad that most definitely is not keto friendly or gluten free and I'll track down our author."

I left Nancy and made my way through a crowd that seemed cheerful and happy in spite of the disappearance of our guest speaker. On my way to the backstage area, I popped into one of the bathrooms just to make sure Luanne wasn't holed up in one of them, having a reaction to accidently ingested donuts or something.

Luanne wasn't there, but I nearly plowed into Eva. The woman had her purse half in the sink and was reapplying her lipstick, a few damp paper towels by her purse. She looked exhausted.

"Almost over," I told her. "Hang in there."

"Almost over for you." She stared into the mirror. "Only the beginning of my problems for me."

"I hate to add to them, but do you know where Luanne is? We need her for the photo op as people leave."

She shrugged. "Haven't seen her, but I've been backstage dealing with issues and handling work e-mails for the last hour. Maybe she went back to the bed and breakfast? That crazy fan woman really shook her up, and on top of the run-in with Star earlier and the thing with Sebastian, she was pretty raw."

"I don't think she would have walked far in those heels." I pivoted to leave, then hesitated, curiosity getting the best of me as always. "What was up with the producer guy? Something wrong with the film deal?"

She turned to me, her smile wan. "The usual legal crap. We'll get it all sorted. That's why we have lawyers, right?"

Yeah, I guessed so. "Well, if you see Luanne, tell her to go up front and find Nancy."

I headed out and checked two more bathrooms. Not finding the author there, I descended the stairs to the left of the stage area and scooted through the door. There were a few dressing rooms for when the theater was putting on plays or live performances. One had been set up for Luanne's use. She'd retreated there after the incident with the knife-woman, so I figured she might have once again gone there for a private moment.

I knocked and waited, then pressed my ear against the door. Barging in on Luanne Trainor while she was buck naked changing clothing wasn't something I wanted to experience.

"Ms. Trainor?" I knocked again. When there was no response, I turned the handle and slowly eased the door open, half expecting an indignant shriek. The room was empty. The bowl of fruit appeared to be untouched, the half-empty bottle of water still on the dressing table. Maybe she'd decided to call it a night and gone back to the B&B as Eva had suggested. Although I couldn't imagine her hoofing it five blocks on those heels of hers. She'd probably complained the entire way about how Milford didn't have a decent taxi service, and that someone should have called her an Uber.

I was about to leave when I noticed Luanne's briefcase on the floor next to the dressing table, and her purse beside the chair. Surely she wouldn't have gone back to the B&B without her purse at the very least?

"Ms. Trainor? Luanne?" I checked behind the dressing screen and did another quick sweep of the small room, worried that maybe she was passed out or something, but the author wasn't there.

She had to be *somewhere* in the theater. Unless she'd been kidnapped. I immediately imagined a car full of masked women pulling up to the back entrance and storming through the fire door to slap a pillowcase over Luanne's head and drag her away. It was a fantastical—and very unlikely—scenario, but I figured I should probably check the fire door anyway. It was propped open with the brick again. I scooted through the opening and up the four grimy cement steps to the long, narrow passageway that separated the theater from the six-story office building beside it. The office building had a fire door of their own about six feet down, and I was willing to bet that one was locked from the inside and alarmed, not that I expected our speaker to be wandering around a vacant building that was home to two insurance companies, an accounting firm, and six law offices. At one end, the passageway spilled into the sidewalk and street in front of the theater. At the other end, it bypassed the city parking deck and opened up to a narrow roadway. Along its length were a few other fire doors, and an opening with a series of steps that led into the parking garage. I headed that way, although I was pretty sure my chances of finding Luanne were slim to none. She didn't strike me as the sort of person who stepped out into a narrow alley for a smoke, and why should she sneak out this way to head back to her B&B when going out the front door would put her a block closer?

And why hadn't she taken her purse or briefcase?

I eyed the theater through the slit of the propped-open fire door, hoping I didn't return to find it shut and locked, forcing me to walk all the way around the building to the front door. Then I headed down the a long path toward the road that ran along the back of the theater, pausing at the steps to the parking garage.

Something prickled in the back of my neck. I spun around and saw a shadow out of the corner of my eye. Holt. Or rather, Holt's ghost.

"You're not supposed to be here." I shook my finger at the shadow. "Only when I'm working, remember? That was our deal. I'm not working, so go away and come back Monday morning."

I wished the guy would get lost, because this was getting to be annoying. Could I take a restraining order out on a ghost? I doubted that I knew anyone who did exorcisms, or whatever it took to get rid of pesky spirits. Maybe I could have Daisy recommend someone to craft that amulet, because I was starting to change my mind on that whole thing.

Holt brushed past me with a prickle of arctic chill, then floated up the stairs. I followed him, more because I was planning on giving the garage a quick glance than any hope that Holt's ghost would lead me to Luanne.

A ghost bloodhound. Now *that* would be useful.

"Ms. Trainor?" I called as I topped the steps. The parking garage was rather full for a Saturday evening, no doubt a combination of late-reservation diners in downtown Milford and those who were attending the speaker series.

There was an echoing silence that greeted my shout. I turned around to leave and nearly jumped out of my skin as the automated parking validation machine loudly announced that I should pay for my parking voucher before returning to my car as the exits were only able to accept credit card payments. I clasped a hand to my chest and took a few breaths. Luanne had probably already returned to the meet-and-greet and here I was traipsing down narrow alleyways and parking garages when I could have been eating organic kale chips and sipping cheap champagne.

As I turned to head down the stairs I saw Holt's ghost hovering at the end of a row of SUVs, next to the stairwell that led up to the remaining five floors of the parking garage and the small set of stairs that led to the back exit. Normally I would have been happy to leave him in the parking garage, hoping that he'd decided to make it his new home, but there was something about the shadow—something that again sent the hairs on the back of my neck to prickling attention.

Hesitating for a few seconds, I slowly made my way toward the ghost, catching my breath when I saw a pair of high-heeled shoes sticking out at the edge of the back tire of one of the SUVs. The heels were connected to feet and legs, and to the sprawled form of Luanne Trainor.

CHAPTER 11

I ran to her, fumbling in my pocket for my cell phone, not sure whether dialing 911 took precedence over administering CPR. As I reached the woman, it was clear where my priorities should lie.

I dialed 911. Then I turned my back on Luanne as I spoke to the dispatch lady. Holt's shadow had retreated to hover near an old Miata a few cars down, but another shadow was forming just at the edge of my vision, by the…by the body.

The dispatch lady told me to remain at the scene until the police arrived. I'd planned on doing that anyway, mainly because I was afraid someone else would stumble upon this horrible sight. The meet-and-greet was wrapping up. Some people might decide to forgo the photo op and head home, and some of those people might have parked in the garage. Besides…

I slowly turned around, steeling myself for a repeat glimpse of the woman I'd just been talking to not an hour before. Her one shoe was half off her foot, the other twisted at the ankle. There was blood, but from the weird angle of her head… The shadow had moved closer, hovering over Luanne's legs and feet like a dark fog. *Her* ghost. *Her* spirit.

"I'm sorry," I told her. There was nothing I could do—nothing but wait here for the first responders and hope no one came out of the theater and saw…. Once again, my gaze drifted to her head twisted in an unnatural angle.

I shifted my eyes back down to her shoes—a safer place to look. Had she fallen? Hit her head on the step and broken her neck? We were at the lower floor of the parking garage and she was just at the bottom of the steps that headed up to the street—all of three steps. Surely someone couldn't die from falling down three steps? Could they?

It was a parking garage, full of concrete everything. And Luanne was wearing those stupid high-heeled platform shoes. Which begged another question—what the heck was she doing here? Not just here in the parking garage, but down at this end? Had she stepped in here for a quiet place to smoke? But why walk to the far end of the garage in impractical footwear? This exit wasn't leading to the street she'd take if she decided to walk back to the B&B. There wasn't anything outside this exit except the back end of a Mexican restaurant and a few dumpsters. The narrow street at this exit was practically an alleyway. It ran along the service entrances of some downtown businesses, ending on Main Street at one side and Mullaney on the other. Did Luanne have a sudden desire to grab some tacos and figured she'd take a shortcut? I envisioned Luanne climbing the cement steps with her insane shoes, missing a step or catching a narrow heel in something and….

Falling backward. But she wasn't positioned like she should have been if she'd fallen while climbing the stairs. She was facedown. Or would have been facedown if…

Nope. Not going to think about that.

Maybe her foot had slipped on something—a greasy

smear of food someone had dropped and not bothered to clean up. If her foot had shot backward out from under her, then she would have pitched forward.

And be laying on top of the stairs. Even if she'd slid down a few, she shouldn't be all the way down at the bottom of the steps. I risked a quick glance and noticed that the blood wasn't on any of the stairs except the bottom one, so that theory wasn't plausible either. Maybe the greasy taco smear was on the floor? Judging by her position, it did look like she'd fallen forward onto the bottom step from the landing. I looked at the area around her feet. Although the concrete was stained and pitted, I didn't see anything that would explain a slip.

Broken shoe heel? Her ghost certainly seemed interested in her shoes, so I bent over Luanne's feet, eyeing the narrow red heels of her creamy patent-leather pumps. They looked expensive, well-made, and the heels seemed to be firmly affixed to the rest of the shoe. Although I couldn't imagine anyone being able to walk in those things. I'd break my neck taking two steps in them. Although that wasn't a visual I really wanted in my head at this time.

I'd straightened from my perusal of Luanne's shoes and started at the sound of a footstep, turning to keep whoever it was away from the crime scene, but the person behind me wasn't one of the ladies from the meet-and-greet. It was a boy.

Well, a man actually, although sometime in the last decade I'd taken to considering any male under the age of thirty to be a 'boy'." He looked to be in his early twenties. He was average height and slight of build with a long, thin face. He had dark brown hair that flopped over his eyes in the current fashion among young people. He was wearing a long black cape.

There's something decidedly chilling about a man in a

cape. A woman wearing one looks charmingly vintage, as if she's stepped out of a Victorian novel or some PBS miniseries. A man in a cape conjures up imagines of Phantom of the Opera, Jack the Ripper, or someone practicing the dark arts. Although it would be very peculiar for someone to be conjuring devils on a Saturday night in downtown Milford, let alone searching the parking deck for their car afterward. If they could conjure underworld spirits, I'd like to think they would have some supernatural means of finding their cars, like a magic GPS amulet or something, not wandering around with a key fob in their hands.

And clearly the day's events cumulating with the dead body at my feet and driven me insane to be considering such things with a wide-eyed man before me, cape or no cape.

"Um, the police are on their way," I told him, partially to reassure him and partially to warn him, because he still might be Jack the Ripper for all I knew.

"She wasn't supposed to *stab* her," Caped Man said, his voice rising about three octaves in pitch. "I told her this was a bad idea. I told her…" The man suddenly looked up at me, a whole host of emotions in his face. Then with a panicked noise, he whirled about and raced away, his cape flying behind him.

"Wait!" I called out, not because I particularly wanted to hang out with maybe-Jack-the-Ripper, but because I was sure the police would want to question him. Although I was about to go running after him. The police dispatch lady had told me to stay with the body. Besides, there was no way I could run fast enough to catch that man, even wearing my sensible shoes.

What he'd said, though… Who wasn't supposed to stab Luanne? Had she been stabbed? I glanced quickly at the body beside me. There was a lot of blood. If she'd been stabbed in the chest, I wouldn't be able to see it from this angle. Maybe that young man's lady friend had stabbed Luanne, and she'd hit her head on the step as she'd fallen?

Although that didn't make sense, because I had a good idea who that man's lady friend might be. Jack the Ripper and the Phantom of the Opera weren't the only men who wore capes. Vampires did. Specifically, the vampire Roman from the Fanged Darkness novels.

Not that I thought the slim, floppy-haired boy in the parking garage was really a vampire. The crazy fan with a knife had said Roman was patrolling the area for ghouls. I'd thought that was just her wild imaginings in her I'm-the-heroine-Trelanie fantasy, but maybe not. Maybe this weird reenactment had included an actual living, breathing male who was supposed to roam around the theater and the block surrounding it, dressed in a cape, guarding against ghouls.

If that young man was the crazy fan's Roman, then his fears were unfounded. His partner-in-imagination hadn't stabbed Luanne, because she'd been hauled into police custody while Luanne was still living and breathing, her knife confiscated. Even if she'd been released—which I doubted, given how slowly things moved at the station—they wouldn't have given her back the knife, and she wouldn't have had time to return here and stab Luanne in a parking deck. Would she?

The sound of engines echoed off the concrete walls and I saw two police cars and an ambulance make their way around the turns to where I stood. I waited until they had parked and exited their cars before approaching.

"You Kay Carrera?" A uniformed officer approached me while the other cops got busy roping off the immediate area of the parking garage. A woman with a camera began snapping photos.

"Yes, I'm Kay Carrera, the one who found her and called it in." I shook the man's outstretched hand. Poor guy to be out on a Saturday night like this. I guess the rookies got the crappy shifts. And I was pretty sure he was a rookie because he was young—young enough to fall into my 'boy' category. Under twenty-five, by my reckoning.

"I'm Officer Raoul Gonzales," he told me. Officer Gonzales had the bold direct eye contact, the self-assured stance, the firm grip of every police officer I'd ever met—even the ones who stopped in our office to shoot the bull with J.T. and grab whatever pastries I'd brought in for the day. His dark hair was barely a shadow on his head, his face freshly shaven. There was a little scar at the corner of his eye, something old that had probably needed stitches but hadn't received them. He was a good-looking man, the type you'd call in an emergency, the type you'd feel safe with in a dark alley at night, or a parking garage at night next to a dead body. If he'd encountered the vampire Roman in the pursuit of justice, my money would have been on Officer Gonzales.

Pulling a notepad from his pocket, the officer led me over to his car and graciously allowed me to sit in the passenger seat with the door open as I told him everything that had happened, including all my theories about the possibility that Luanne's choice in footwear had led to her death.

"Probably just an unlucky fall," he agreed as he scribbled on the notepad. "We'll have to treat it as suspicious until the M.E. says otherwise, though."

I dug a card out of my pocket and handed it to him. "If you need anything further, let me know."

He glanced at it, then looked up at me in surprise. "You work for Pierson? Hey, you're that skip tracer of his that figured out the football player murder, aren't you? Miles Pickford told me you're pretty smart. And that you make really good muffins."

It was nice to know I had a fan at the Locust Point police force, and that Miles had been spreading the word of my skills and my baking prowess. "That's me. Not that I'll be of any help in an accidental death, but just in case it turns into something more, please pass my information along to the detective. I spent the last few days as the event liaison to Ms. Trainor, so I might be able to provide some insight."

He nodded, pocketing my card. "Will do. You're free to leave, Ms. Carrera. Just duck under the tape to the left there."

To the left was where a group of onlookers had gathered, Holt's ghost still present and lurking at the outskirts of the crowd. A quick glance backward told me that Luanne's ghost was still hovering over by her shoes—which she'd probably continue to do until they eventually removed them from her body. The spirit didn't seem angry, just agitated and stressed. Her shadowy form wasn't as sharp as Holt's ghost, giving me the feeling that she wouldn't be staying around for long. Which would be a relief since Holt's ghost showed no signs of leaving.

I headed for the police tape and the others. Nancy stood at the front, her hands fluttering wildly, her face twisted in distress. Eva beside her stared, numb, as if she couldn't quite believe it. Everyone else seemed equally horrified and curious about what had happened to our guest of honor. I slid under the tape and Nancy moved over to make a place for me between her and the agent.

"Did she have any next of kin we should contact?" I asked Eva. "Someone who would want to fly in and make arrangements?"

The woman shook her head as if clearing the fog from it. "I think there's a brother in Chicago. Greg, or something? She only mentioned him in passing. I don't know if they were close or anything."

"Would someone at your agency know?" I pressed. "An editor at the publishing house? The police will probably check her phone, but I thought if we could call someone...it might be easier coming from someone who knew her rather than the police."

Eva took out her phone and stared down at it. "No one's going to be at the agency or publishing company until Monday morning. There might be something on her travel profile, though. I'll call my assistant and have her look it up."

The agent turned and squeezed her way past the onlookers, dialing her phone then putting it up to her ear.

"Poor woman." Nancy's voice was agitated and breathless.

"It's shocking," the woman next to her agreed. "What was she doing out in the garage?"

"Getting in her car and skipping out early on the reception, that's what," another woman chimed in. "I thought she'd be nicer. Or at least put some effort into acting like she wanted to be here. Not that I want to see anyone die, but she was kind of a jerk."

"Oh, no! Had she finished the last few books in the series yet?" the first woman's voice edged toward panic. "What if we never find out what happened to Trelanie and Roman?"

"They kill all the ghouls and ride off into the moonrise together, that's what happens. And she didn't have a rental car, so she wasn't here skipping out early on the meet-and-greet unless she planned on hobbling all the way to the B&B in those shoes."

I turned in relief to hear Daisy's voice behind me.

"She was probably grabbing a smoke and fell," I said to the crowd in general. "Those heels…it's a wonder she could walk at all on those things."

Everyone nodded and murmured in agreement. Except Daisy.

"She *smoked*? All that gluten-free, organic, probiotic stuff and she *smoked*?"

I shrugged. "Maybe? Everyone has a vice."

"Maybe she was taking a shortcut to the Mexican place,"

Daisy conjectured. "I don't blame her for sneaking out for some tacos. Besides your icebox cake and the ham salad, the food at that meet-and-greet was appalling. Who eats that kind of stuff? Rice flour and bean paste and Brussel sprout sandwiches? The most tasteless stuff I've ever had."

"Why subject us all to the gluten-free, organic, probiotic stuff and sneak out for tacos?" I countered. "That's as much of a stretch as the idea of her smoking."

The reason for that tasteless stuff had been Luanne's strict diet. Had the woman been cheating on her self-imposed food regime, sneaking out for a taco as Daisy suggested?

"Taking a phone call?" I suggested. "One that she absolutely didn't want anyone else to overhear?"

"Then she finished it and put the phone back in her pocket before she tripped," Daisy pointed out. "Or her phone would have been smashed on the ground beside her."

"That's plausible." More plausible than Luanne smoking or sneaking out for a taco, anyway. But who would she have been calling on a Saturday night? Her agent was right here, and business stuff would have had to wait until Monday anyway. Suddenly my imagination was running wild with the thoughts of Luanne calling a secret boyfriend.

The paramedics loaded the body into the ambulance, the ghost right along with the body, and the crowd began to disperse. I waited with Daisy and Nancy, watching as the police did their final pictures. With Luanne's sprawled form removed, it *did* look as though she'd pitched forward onto the bottom step. I winced, thinking of how horrible that must have been. Hopefully it had been quick and painless.

"Do you need a lift back to your car?" Daisy asked me. "Or are you parked by the theater?"

I turned to look at Eva, who was still talking on her phone and pacing back and forth in front of the payment machine. I wouldn't need to come in to take Luanne to the airport tomorrow, but I did owe the B&B owners an explanation as to why one of their guests would not be returning. Eva could tell them, but I was the coordinator for Luanne, and I felt it would be better coming from me. Besides, I really wanted a few moments alone with the agent.

"I'm parked out in front of the theater, but I need to go back to the inn first. Eva's staying there. I'll walk with her or call Gene and ask him to pick us up." I looked down at my sensible flats, then over at the modest heels the agent wore. "The walk will probably do us good, though."

"You sure?" My friend eyed me with concern. "You seem pretty calm now but coming upon someone like this has got to be a shock."

A shock I should be getting used to. How many dead bodies had I come across in the last five months? This was getting ridiculous.

"I'll be fine, I promise. Yoga tomorrow? I don't exactly have to get up early to go to the airport anymore."

"Yoga," Daisy agreed. "And this time I'll bring breakfast. Real breakfast. Bacon and eggs, and more gluten than a bread factory."

I couldn't help but smile. "Deal."

Daisy left, and Nancy headed back to the theater once she was sure I would be fine on my own. I made my way over to Eva as the woman hung up her phone and stared down at it with slumped shoulders. A shadow formed to her right over by the payment machine, slowly creeping forward to hover over the agent like a foggy photo filter. It seemed Luanne's ghost had abandoned her shoes in favor of the location of her death. The agent shivered, put her phone in her pocket, and rubbed her arms.

"Walk back to the B&B with me?" I asked her. "I figured

you could use some company and I need to talk to Gene and Paula anyway."

She nodded, giving me a wan smile. "Thanks. I'd feel kind of creepy walking on my own, especially after everything that just happened. Do you think we can get back into the theater, though? My purse is in there along with a few other things."

Goodness, I hadn't even thought of that. I'd left my purse locked in my car, figuring I'd need both hands free tonight and not wanting to worry about keeping track of it, but I would need to collect my icebox cake dishes and the cooler. Suddenly I remembered the dressing room and realized I should probably gather Luanne's things as well. Should I give them to Eva? The police? Ask Gene to hold them for when this brother or whoever came in to make arrangements?

"Nancy is probably over there by now." I led the way up into the sidewalk passageway between the two buildings, but someone had moved the brick and closed the fire door. We walked around to the front where, thankfully, the caterers were still moving tables and warming trays out and into a large cargo van. One of them recognized me and nodded me in where I found Nancy standing in what had been our reception hall.

"We're here to get purses and stuff," I told Nancy.

"I've got your cooler and dishes over here," she told me. "Can I have a moment, Eva? I've got a few things here I need to ask you about in light of...in light of what happened."

The agent glanced toward the stage area and hesitated.

"I'll get your purse," I told her. "It's in the dressing room with Luanne's stuff?"

Again, I sensed her reluctance. "Yes. I just...I need to get Luanne's purse and briefcase as well. We shouldn't leave it here."

"I was thinking of that, too." I patted her on the arm. "I'll grab it all and meet you here."

She smiled. "Thanks. Be careful with the briefcase. Luanne might have some confidential stuff in there. Contracts and things. Don't want any of them left behind."

Why would Luanne have been carting around confidential documents in hard copy in a briefcase that she carelessly left in an unlocked dressing room? I hoped they weren't national secrets or anything, although when it came to fans of her books, I could completely imagine someone trying to sneak backstage and take a quick look to see if there was an early edition of the next novel they could sell on one of those torrent sites.

The dressing room looked just as forlorn as it had before. I eyed the flowers sadly, thinking I should grab them and take them down to the B&B or have Nancy take them home. No sense in having them just wilt here unappreciated, waiting for the Monday cleaning crew to toss them in the trash.

Reaching out to touch the velvety crimson petals, I saw a shadow form off to my side. I knew immediately that it wasn't Luanne's ghost but Holt's.

"Why are you here? I've really had enough death and ghosts for the evening. Can you just leave me alone for a few days? Come back Monday when I'm in the office and I'll let you read the latest Creditcorp skip trace file."

The briefcase wobbled and fell over, papers spilling from it.

"Holt! You were going to stop this, right? No rolling potatoes off my counter or other poltergeisting." I stooped to shove the papers back into the case, eyeing them because I'm nosy.

A letter from the production studio demanding a release of rights by noon today or they would revoke their offer.

Eek, was this why that producer's assistant was so upset? Was this what Eva was talking about in the bathroom when she said there were some legal snags? What the heck was the problem? Just sign the darned thing already.

Feeling a twinge of guilt for snooping among a dead woman's belongings, I pushed the letter into the briefcase along with three other ones from the production company demanding that Luanne secure a full release of film rights to the Fanged Darkness series. Each letter had a thick release document attached. The very last page had a spot for signatures and notaries—Luanne's signature and someone named Geraldine Pook.

Okay, so the twinge of guilt was more like a brief fleeting thought. Who was Geraldine Pook and why was Luanne ignoring the right's release papers? Didn't she *want* a film deal? I threw these papers back into the briefcase along with a notebook, a planner, and an old-fashioned address book. Seems Luanne didn't like to rely completely on her phone scheduler or database. Not that I blamed her. I had a hard-copy address book at home as well, although I didn't lug it around with me.

I reached for the last item—a tan envelope. It slid away from me. I crab walked a few steps toward it, only to have it slide away again.

"Holt! Knock it off!" Eva would be here any minute and I'd be mortified if she found me down on the floor with the contents of Luanne's briefcase. She'd think I was snooping, which was totally what I was doing.

I reached again for the envelope and it flipped, papers sliding out of it and across the floor. Okay, now I couldn't help but look, even though I'd planned on not rifling through the contents of the envelope.

It was a manuscript, marked up with comments in red pen. And it wasn't just any manuscript, it was the final

Fanged Darkness novel, the one that was supposed to come out next year. I tried not to read it as I gathered up the papers. Spoilers sucked, as I'd found out yesterday. This must be Luanne's draft, back from the editor at the publishing house and ready for her revisions. Except the notes looked a lot like they were in Luanne's writing. Weird that they weren't doing all of this online in this day and age. And sad that she'd never gotten a chance to do the revisions. Hopefully they'd have someone else who could button up this novel and get it out to the reading public and finish the series off.

It wasn't until I started to slide the manuscript back into the envelope that I realized the address on the front was to this Geraldine Pook, *from* Luanne Trainor.

I was running out of time. Grabbing my phone, I snapped a picture of the address, then looked through Luanne's address book, taking another picture of Geraldine Pook's contact info. Then I took a few quick pictures of some random pages of the manuscript before shoving it all back into the envelope and into the briefcase.

I *was* nosy. And curious. Even more curious because a few peculiar things were beginning to be made clear.

CHAPTER 12

Eva was silent as we walked back to the B&B, both hers and Luanne's purses over her shoulder and the woman's briefcase in one hand. When Gene let us in, her gaze drifted up the staircase.

"Guess I should go pack her things," she said, her voice numb.

"Are you flying out tomorrow? Do you need a lift to the airport?" I asked.

She shook her head. "I need to stay until Monday or Tuesday to see what the publisher wants to do and wait for Luanne's brother to make arrangements for her...body. Press statements. And we'll need to make an announcement about the final books in the series."

"Had she written them yet?" I asked, pretending I hadn't seen the manuscript in the briefcase.

"The series will finish out," she assured me. "And there will be other books as well. I just need to talk to the publisher first and get things squared away."

"And the film deal?" I eyed her closely, watching for her reaction.

She shrugged. "There were some legal issues that hadn't been completely buttoned up. The producer is a bit gun shy, but nothing sells books like a dead author. They'll see the money and come running."

"Did she have a will? If the estate is tied up in probate, that might complicate your already hairy legal issues on film rights," I told her.

She shot me a tight smile. "Luanne sold full rights to the publisher. She's out of the loop. All her estate needs to do is collect a check."

"Then what were the legal issues?" I pressed.

"Some silly things that I'm sure will be worked out in the next few weeks." Eva set the briefcase down and extended a hand. "Thanks for your help this weekend, Kay. I'll send you a special edition of book seven when it releases next week, if you'd like."

Clearly a dismissal. "Thanks, I'd really love that. It was good meeting you."

I watched her climb the stairs then turned to Gene and Paula who had been lurking just inside the dining area. I wasn't the only nosy one in the county, it seemed.

"We heard about Ms. Trainor," Paula whispered, coming into the room with her husband close behind her.

News traveled fast. Milford might be larger than Locust Point, but it still had all the hallmarks of a small town.

"Yes, it was quite a shock to find her there in the parking garage," I told them.

Paula's eyes widened. "*You* found her? Oh, Kay! Come in the kitchen with us and I'll make you a nice hot cup of tea. You poor thing."

I found myself bustled along, even though I protested that I really needed to be getting home. It really was very sweet of Paula to offer me tea, but I realized before my feet hit the tile floor of the kitchen that she had a bit of an ulterior motive.

"We billed the speaker series for tonight as well. It's nonrefundable..." She put the kettle on and shot me a nervous glance. "Not to be crude or anything, but I'm assuming her things are going to remain in her room at least overnight."

"I'll say something to Nancy, but I'm sure right now she's got more to worry about than whether the event is paying for tonight's room or not."

Paula winced, putting a cup and a selection of loose herbal teas in front of me. "What do you think happened to her?"

I shrugged. "Fell? You saw those crazy shoes she liked to wear. It looked like she hit her head on the step. A freak accident."

"Couldn't have happened to a nicer person," Gene drawled.

"Gene!" Paula gasped.

"She wasn't exactly pleasant to either of you two," I said. "Actually, she wasn't pleasant to anyone."

"Especially that assistant of hers," Paula added. "Gene and I...well, Ms. Trainor was only going to be here a few days, so it wasn't too hard to turn the other cheek. I feel bad for that assistant woman, having to work with her every day, putting up with her rudeness and abuse."

"Assistant?" I frowned. "You mean Eva? Her agent? I think that's a bit of an even relationship as far as the power dynamic goes. She's in charge of selling Luanne's books and negotiating the terms and conditions of those deals. Plus, she's got a contract. It's not like Luanne can just fire her or anything."

"Didn't seem like much of an even relationship," Gene commented. "Kinda hard when your crazy client provides ninety percent of your salary, don't you think? Then that woman comes back and the two of them practically get into a brawl in the front parlor… Surprised that agent didn't just let them beat the tar out of each other."

"Wait. What woman?"

"After the brunch," Paula explained, pouring the hot water into a little teapot and placing it in front of me. "The one with the diaper bag as a purse. The one that was upset about the character getting killed off. She came back, and I didn't think anything about it when I called Ms. Trainor to come down for a guest."

"Don't think Ms. Trainor would have bothered seeing her, but the woman had a gift." Gene grinned. "Seems our author really likes gifts."

"Not that kind of gift, she didn't." Paula shot her husband a scowl. "It was a cow heart. Who gives someone a cow heart?"

I selected my tea and poured the hot water over the strainer. "Someone who is upset about Barton Wells being killed off, that's who. Eva told me that there were all sorts of hate mail and that they'd gotten a cow heart delivered last year as well. I guess a fan group got together and decided that was the best way to protest the death of a fictional character."

"Well, Ms. Trainor threw it across the room and next thing I know they're wrestling and yanking hair and screaming at each other. That Eva woman ran downstairs and pulled them apart. Made Luanne go up to her room and offered the girl an early release or something to keep quiet about it. Then later on, the two of them are the ones having a screaming match in the parlor."

Poor Eva. I drank down my tea and stood up, thanking Paula and Gene for their hospitality and reassuring them that I'd speak to Nancy about the fee for tonight's room. On my way back to the theater and my car, I texted Nancy and asked her for the guest list at brunch—particularly inquiring about the young woman who'd had the burping cloth over her shoulder when she'd come in. The theater was closed up and dark when I got in my car and Nancy was clearly long gone, but she must have still been awake because I got a text with a PDF attachment before I'd left the city limits.

By the time I pulled in my driveway it was well after midnight. The porch light was still on, as was the one in the upstairs hallway, and the kitchen. I appreciated Judge Beck making sure I didn't come home to a dark house, and I especially appreciated my furry friend racing to greet me as I came through the door. I set down my cooler with the empty pans and scooped up my cat so he could bump my chin with his head and nestle against my neck with a rumbling purr.

"Exciting night?"

My heart nearly left my chest. Looking up, I saw Judge Beck in the kitchen doorway in his pajamas with reading glasses perched on his nose and a cup of something in his hand.

"You have no idea. What are you doing still up?"

He raised the mug. "Couldn't sleep so I made a pot of chamomile. Want some? You can join me in the kitchen and we'll discuss prune juice and how those darned kids won't stay off our lawn."

I really loved having a roommate. I loved having *this* roommate. Yes, Taco was the main man in my life right now, but it was nice to have actual human companionship as well.

"Tea sounds lovely." I walked into the kitchen with Taco still in my arms and sat on a stool while Judge Beck pulled out another mug and poured the tea. He held up the sugar with a raised eyebrow, but I waved it away, figuring I didn't need it with the sweetness of the chamomile, or at this hour of the night.

"More craziness with the author?" he asked, putting the mug in front of me and sliding onto the other stool. "I'll bet you're dreading the trip to the airport tomorrow. Maybe you can just open the door and kick her out of it without stopping."

"I won't be taking her to the airport tomorrow because she's dead," I blurted out. Then I took a sip of the blissfully hot tea. It wasn't as fancy as what I'd had at Paula's, but somehow this tasted so much better here in my home, with a person, and a cat, I cared about around me.

Judge Beck choked on his tea, then pounded his chest as he coughed. I waited for him to catch his breath, calmly sipping from my mug. Maybe I was still in shock. Maybe it had all settled and I was just numb. Maybe discovering so many dead bodies in the last few months had jaded me to the whole experience.

"You. Said. Dead?" the judge sputtered.

"Dead. And that probably wasn't the worst part of my day."

He took a ragged breath, another sip of tea, and leaned forward. "Do tell."

"Remember the brunch that started okay, but then someone brought up a beloved character that Luanne inadvisably killed off? Remember I said she went off on these fans who'd paid some big money to have a private brunch with her? And that the rest of the brunch was tense and awkward? Well, evidently, one of them was angry enough to return with a cow heart in a box and Eva had to break up an actual, physical fight between Luanne and the fan. Then at the main event, some other author who'd had a plagiarism lawsuit against Luanne was there and stood up, loudly reasserting her claims. Then some whacko fan with a knife showed up at the meet-and-greet and needed to be carted off by the police. Then Luanne disappeared, kind of understandably because she might have been struggling to get through the rest of the event after having some woman point a knife at her. When I went to find her, I found her dead in the city garage."

He stared, openmouthed. After a few seconds, he shook his head and took another gulp of tea. "Holy cow, that sounds like it should be a soap opera. Or the plot of one of her novels. Not that I've read any of her novels."

"I've got some if you want to give them a go," I told him. "They're really good but get ready for some cold showers."

He grimaced. "I'll skip it, thanks. I've had enough cold showers during the last year. No need to further torture myself."

This was.... well, it was a really weird conversation to be having with my roommate, who I had platonic feelings of affection for. Strictly platonic. Although this particular subject reminded me of that nagging suspicion I'd had ever since I'd seen that manuscript in Luanne's briefcase.

"Actually, I'm beginning to believe that Luanne didn't write those books." I gave him a knowing nod. "I read some of her earlier stuff and it's *nothing* like her bestselling series. Then tonight I went to get her briefcase from the dressing room, and a manuscript fell out. It was the last Fanged Darkness novel, and Luanne had marked it all up and was sending it to some woman named Geraldine Pook."

The judge shook his head. "A side editor, maybe? A friend who pre-reads and gives her feedback?"

"I don't know." I narrowed my eyes. "I wonder if she doesn't have a ghostwriter."

"A lot of people have ghostwriters," the judge pointed out. "It seems like every one of those political thriller novels is some kind of ghostwritten collaboration. That big-name bestseller with the television commercials? I envision a sweatshop of ink-stained writers, frantically typing on laptops in a dimly lit warehouse, churning out his novels for him."

I laughed, knowing exactly who he meant. "What if there were some sort of issue with the ghostwriter, though? What if this Geraldine Pook found out there was a million-dollar film deal going down and decided she was getting the short end of the stick? What if she came to Milford to demand that Luanne give her more money, and they argued, and she pushed Luanne—"

"First off, the woman fell," Judge Beck interrupted. "It was an accident. You yourself said she could hardly walk in those shoes, and from what I remember, that parking garage has got enough cracks to make the most surefooted person stumble. Secondly, ghostwriters have contracts. The publishing houses make sure those people are locked in tight legally. It's work-for-hire. Geraldine Pook writes the book, gets a paycheck, and owns nothing of the rights on that work."

"But she's bitter and angry because when she signed on to write these, she never envisioned they'd hit number one on the New York Times list or get a big-name film deal. So she decides to confront Luanne. Maybe she knows something about the author. Maybe she can blackmail her for a percentage of the film deal."

"Maybe you're the one who should be writing fiction novels," Judge Beck countered with a grin.

I sighed, looking down at my tea. "You're right. It's probably all on the up-and-up with this Geraldine Pook, even if she is a ghostwriter for Luanne Trainor. I'm sure the publishing company has handled this sort of arrangement before, and for all I know the ghostwriter is a professional who has been freelancing for decades behind the scenes."

"And even if that's not the case, Luanne Trainor fell by accident." Judge Beck motioned to my mug with his own with a teasing smile. "Now drink up and go to bed before you start imagining all sorts of other wild conspiracies involving poisoned cow hearts or gangs of ghouls roaming the Milford parking garage."

CHAPTER 13

Sweat trickled down the back of my neck, detouring along my collarbone and pooling at the edge of my sports bra as my body shook from the plank pose. Dratted Daisy. She'd had us holding this thing forever and muscles I didn't know I had were screaming.

"What if someone actually killed Luanne Trainor?"

My friend's voice was even and strong. I, on the other hand, could only manage a grunt in reply.

"Seriously," she continued. "That crazy-pants woman with the knife can't have been the only nut job prowling around. Or plagiarism woman. After what you told me about the brunch, I did some internet browsing and found a ton of fan sites, some of which are devoted to expressing how upset they are about Barton Wells's death and doing anything they can to force Luanne into resurrecting him."

I grunted in reply. Then sighed in relief as Daisy moved into a downward dog.

"What if those brunch ladies posted what Luanne said about never bringing Barton back, and someone decided to express their anger in a more physical way?"

"One came back," I gasped. "Amy Shep. Brought a cow heart. Had a fight."

"*What?*" Daisy jerked her head to look at me. "Who? What?"

I took a breath and followed Daisy into a Parsvottanasana. "One of those Barton Wells fans was at the brunch. She came back and confronted Luanne. Had a cow heart in a box. They had a scuffle. Eva broke it up."

"See? That woman came back once more. She knew no one would allow her into the meet-and-greet after fighting with Luanne, so she waited and accosted her in the parking garage—"

"Oh yeah, because it was just a matter of time until Luanne went out the fire exit and into the parking garage where she didn't even have a car parked and tottered all the way to the back entrance on those crazy high heels. It's not likely, Daisy. Luanne fell. I don't know what she was doing in that garage, but she fell."

Daisy shifted into an Uttanasana. "Well, I think there's foul play. I don't think she fell. Or if she did, she was pushed."

I grimaced, hoping we'd be upright in the next pose. "I'll ask J.T. what the gossip is on Monday," I huffed. "But I'm pretty sure the police on the scene were calling it an accident."

"Well, it couldn't have happened to a nicer person," Daisy grumbled, moving into tree pose.

"Daisy!" I scolded, mirroring her movements with relief. We continued our yoga in silence for a few moments, then I couldn't help but voice my suspicions. "I don't think Luanne actually wrote the Fanged Darkness series herself. Or Infernal Awakenings. I think she was using a ghostwriter."

"What?" Daisy lost her balance on the tree pose, nearly landing on her face. "Was that what the plagiarism thing was all about?"

"No, I think that's something different." I told Daisy all about the old series Luanne had written as well as the manuscript in the briefcase while she regained her position.

"Wow. That's.... that's not technically illegal, but in my opinion it's really immoral. Here everyone is thinking she's one of the best writers in the last three decades and it wasn't even her."

"Lots of people have ghostwriters," I told Daisy as we stood into mountain pose. "Not everyone credits them, either."

"Yeah, but they're all celebrities and politicians—nobody expects them to be writing their own stuff. But other books? It's not ethical at all."

"I'm sure this woman is making good money for her work, and maybe she doesn't want the fame. Although I did wonder if that was the reason for some of the legal issues around the film deal."

"The film deal is off?"

"I got the impression it was on the rocks," I told her as we finished up in prayer pose.

"Huh. So maybe the producer killed Luanne because his career was hinging on this deal and the ghostwriter thing screwed it up. Or maybe Eva killed her because the ghost-writer thing screwed it up. Or maybe a Barton Wells fan killed her, or the plagiarism accuser, or—"

"Or she caught her absurdly tall and pointy heels in a crack in the parking garage floor and fell headfirst onto a concrete step and died completely by accident."

We headed into the house and I poured us both a cup of coffee, pulling the quiche Daisy had brought out of the oven, and a bowl of mixed fruit out of the fridge.

"Let's Google her," Daisy suggested as she grabbed plates and silverware.

"Google Luanne? Or the fan groups? I thought you already did that."

"No, the ghostwriter."

"Daisy, that's creepy." Not that I hadn't contemplated doing just that. I was just as nosy as my best friend.

"Maybe she's an actual author and is just doing this on the side or something. If that's the case, then I totally want to read her other stuff."

That was a pretty valid, non-creepy reason. And I agreed with Daisy—if this Geraldine Pook had written other books, I wanted to read them as well. I pushed the quiche over to Daisy to serve and went into the foyer, returning with my laptop. While Daisy dished out the breakfast, I sipped my coffee and searched the internet.

Luckily, I had Geraldine Pook's address from the envelope and Luanne's address book because the woman wasn't easy to find. Unless she was publishing under an alias, or only acted as a ghostwriter, she didn't have any other books out. She also had no social media accounts or webpage, which seemed odd to me. I'd done freelance work in the past to help make ends meet after Eli's accident, and it was hard to get the word out without some sort of internet presence. Although perhaps Geraldine only did this on the side, and only for Luanne. If she was happy with just the one client, she wouldn't need to have a webpage to solicit others. And given the secrecy about it, I doubted Luanne would have allowed herself or her books to be used as a reference of Geraldine's skill.

Finally, I found something. It seemed Geraldine's husband was a pastor at a church, and she was the leader for the family life committee as well as a Sunday school teacher. There was even a picture of her, smiling and surrounded by a hoard of children. I eyed the service time, then my watch.

"Wanna go to church?" I asked Daisy.

"And risk being struck down by lightning?" She chuckled. "Not gonna happen."

"Even to meet the woman who actually wrote the Fanged Darkness series?" I shot Daisy a sideways glance.

Her eyes narrowed. "Okay. That might actually get me in church."

"It's an hour drive to Bayforest. Think you can be church-ready in half an hour?"

She sighed and eyed the few bites of quiche left on her plate. "Only if you're buying lunch afterward. And only if that lunch includes mimosas. If I've got to step foot in a church, I'm going to need an alcoholic beverage immediately afterward."

I closed the laptop shut and pulled the plate from her hand. "Deal. Now get going and hurry up. We've got a service at Bayforest United Church of Christ to attend."

* * *

BAYFOREST. We were halfway there before I realized what had been nagging me since I'd seen Geraldine Pook's address on the envelope with the manuscript in it. When I'd first picked Luanne up from the airport, she'd wanted me to drive her to Bayforest before taking her to the airport. There wasn't much good reason for a complete stranger to want to go to Bayforest, so I assumed she was planning to head there this very morning to speak with who I was assuming was her ghostwriter. She must not have intended a lengthy conversation—just a quick stop-by before catching her flight back to New York. Was the visit to go over that manuscript in Luanne's briefcase in person? Was it to deal with whatever hitch there was with the film rights? Or was it to have a face-to-face about their agreement and the monetary compensation?

This was like throwing darts at a board while blindfolded. I wasn't even sure why Daisy and I were driving an hour to attend a church and possibly get a chance to speak with a woman who might have ghostwritten Luanne Trainor's two bestselling series. We might leave never having seen her, having only enjoyed a pleasant Sunday church service. Well, for me anyway. I was pretty sure Daisy wouldn't enjoy the service at all.

I glanced over at my friend, who had her feet propped on my dashboard, bopping her head to the music blaring from the radio. It was an adventure. It was something fun to do on a Sunday. I was excited about this spur-of-the-moment road trip. If we came home without having met Geraldine, it still was an adventure.

And I couldn't imagine anyone else I'd rather go on this adventure with.

The service was lovely. Reverend Pook was much younger then I'd thought he'd be, and more of the shepherd in terms of his sermon than a fire-and-brimstone preacher. I couldn't see anyone who stood out as his wife, Geraldine, so I decided to take a chance.

"You're new here," the reverend said as he shook my hand and looked back and forth between Daisy and me. "Have you just moved to Bayforest? I hope you put your information in the guest registry. My wife is in charge of the welcoming committee and she likes to bring over a loaf of zucchini bread to new residents."

"Actually, we were hoping to meet your wife, Geraldine." I gave him a hopeful smile. "We live in Locust Point and I believe we share a friend in common."

I winced a bit at calling Luanne Trainor a friend but hauling all the way to a church service in Bayforest seemed a bit excessive for an acquaintance.

Reverend Pook lifted his head to look about. "She should

be up from the Sunday school rooms by now. There she is! In blue over by the stairs." He lifted his hand to wave and a plump woman who radiated grace and contentment smiled and waved back.

I thanked him and stepped aside, surprised to see Daisy take my place and shake the minister's hand. "It was a lovely service and sermon, by the way," she told him.

"Lovely service and sermon?" I teased Daisy as we moved away.

"Absolutely. I didn't catch on fire. Lightning didn't come down out of the sky and strike me dead. Therefore, it was a lovely service and sermon."

It took more of a wait to speak with Geraldine than her husband. The woman was surrounded by children, and several parents took quite a bit of time discussing the coordination of various upcoming family activities. Finally, we had our chance, and the woman turned to us, deep dimples creasing her round face as she smiled.

"You're new! Have you just moved to town? Do you have children? We pride ourselves on our youth programs and would love to see your little ones next Sunday."

"Actually, we were hoping you could spare some time to meet with us," I confessed. "We're from Locust Point and got your name from Luanne Trainor—"

"Oh, my goodness, I'd nearly forgotten!" Her eyes widened and she clasped her hands to her cheeks. "Is she with you? Of course not, she probably had a plane to catch this morning and I told her I couldn't miss Sunday school. Can you come to my house in half an hour? I have the papers, although I didn't have time to see a notary. Are either of you a notary?" Another woman with two beribboned children in tow approached, and Geraldine glanced over at them. "Just come by in half an hour. You've got my address, right? Four Daffodil lane? I'll see you then."

"But I…but we…." My protests were in vain. Geraldine had turned away and was now engaged in animated discussion with the mother of the two girls.

"That woman should be in sales," Daisy told me as we followed the crowd into the parking area. "All that energy and enthusiasm? And that close…. She'd be selling replacement windows right and left. People would be having them installed before they even realized what they'd signed up for."

"Should we go?" I pulled my keys from my purse. "She thinks we work for Luanne and are here as some sort of courier. I feel like we presented ourselves under false pretenses." And I felt particularly badly about that having just walked out of a church service. Nosy gossipy me drew the line somewhere and impersonating an employee of the publishing company Luanne and Geraldine worked for crossed that line.

"Of course we have to go, if only to set her straight and let her know that Luanne died."

The woman had only died last night and although the news was all over Milford within the hour, I doubt it had hit any major news outlets yet. And somehow I also doubted that a woman preparing for several church services this morning had found the time to get on social media and see the trending news of Luanne Trainor's death.

"You're right. We need to tell her." Okay, that was probably an excuse for us to continue being nosy and to find out if Geraldine was really the ghostwriter for the series like I'd suspected. She had to be. Nothing else explained it.

"So…. murderer or not murderer?" Daisy asked as she climbed into my car.

"What?" I eyed her in confusion.

"Geraldine. She doesn't strike me as the type who would drive to Milford to confront Luanne about wanting more money."

"No, she doesn't. And why would she, since she clearly expected Luanne to come see her this morning? It would be easier to just wait for today and ask for more money than haul up to Milford last night. Besides, from what little I know about ghostwriters, the publisher is the one who pays them and contracts them, not the author." I frowned. "At least I think so."

"And the murderer probably isn't her husband either," Daisy continued. "No sense in him going up to Milford last night to off Luanne Trainor when his wife hasn't even had a chance to negotiate a higher salary. Ooh, unless he's one of those controlling types who doesn't want his wife working and did Luanne in so Geraldine no longer had a job outside of the church."

"Daisy, he's a minister!" Besides, Reverend Pook didn't strike me as the sort to take a violent path when a more peaceful option was right in front of him. "And, Luanne's death was an accident, not a murder."

"Hmmm, so you keep saying." Daisy fastened her seatbelt. "Maybe we'll get lucky and this Geraldine will break out some of that zucchini bread. I'm starving."

CHAPTER 14

The door opened and Geraldine stood in the entrance. She'd changed from the blue dress to jeans and a white tank top with a coffee stain down the front. Her dark blonde hair was high on her head in a perky ponytail, and her broad face was creased by two huge dimples. The raucous sounds of children playing and arguing came from behind her.

"Thank you for being patient and waiting for me to finish up at church. Come in, come in! Don't mind the toys or the mess. I set the kids up with a movie downstairs but haven't had a spare second to clean."

"I'm Kay Carrera and this is my friend, Daisy Mercer." I hesitated on the porch. "We're not from the publishing company or to pick up any papers. I just...we just... wanted to meet you. I'm sorry if we're intruding. This is a bad time, clearly."

"Nonsense! Don't be silly. You said you're friends of Luanne's? It's never any bother." The dimples got deeper. "Come in, come in!"

Geraldine Pook ushered us into her house and sat Daisy

and me on a utilitarian, brown micro-suede couch with what looked like several stains and scuff marks on the surface—both old and new.

She disappeared with a flurry of words and energy, then returned with three glasses of sweet tea, only to plop them on a coloring-book-strewn table and vanish again. When she returned the next time, she had a plate of sliced zucchini bread in her hand. Daisy was visibly thrilled.

The place was chaotic. The sounds of high-pitched laughter and shouts came from some other room. There were children's toys scattered across the floor, and a basket of house-decorating magazines on a side table next to a bible. A huge brass crucifix hung over the fireplace mantle next to the iconic blond Jesus picture. A pug yapped at us from the kitchen before turning with a huff to curl up on a navy-blue pillow. If I hadn't known this woman was a minister's wife, I would have thought she took vampire preparedness to a Trelanie level.

"Please call me Gerry," the woman said with a sweet smile. "How is Luanne? I was supposed to get those papers to her weeks ago, but we don't have internet here and my printer died, so I had to drive to Milford to print things off at a Kinkos. These aren't the sorts of things I can use the church printer for, or even the neighbor's. Heaven forbid they found out."

Daisy's eyes about bugged out at the last bit and she shot me one of those looks filled with significance. The woman was right, though. Accidently leaving part of a Fanged Darkness manuscript on a church printer for parishioners to find would be so embarrassing, especially for a minister's wife.

"Although you're not here for the papers, are you?" A frown creased the woman's forehead. "Why are you here? This is supposed to be secret. Luanne insisted, although I didn't exactly want anyone knowing, either. You're friends of hers?"

"No, we're not here for the papers," Daisy spoke up. "Ms. Trainor died unexpectedly, and we thought you should know."

This was a bad idea. Yes, the woman should know, but she'd eventually find out via media. Our being here was beyond nosy at this point. I felt like we were intruding. It wasn't our business if she was ghostwriting the series. That was between her and the publisher and Luanne. I stood and motioned for Daisy to do the same.

"I was the liaison for Ms. Trainor with the speaker series in Milford and saw your name on an envelope with a marked-up manuscript inside and felt you should know firsthand what happened. We'll leave. I'm sure the publisher or Luanne's agent will call you later with details."

"Sit. Sit." She waved a hand at me, her eyes wide with shock. "Luanne is *dead*? When? I just spoke to her Friday. When did this happen?"

"Last night."

Gerry took a deep breath and shook her head. "Was it her heart? She's been so careful about her health since that scare she had ten years ago."

"You knew her that well?" I was more than a bit surprised at her last comment. "You've known her for ten years?"

"Twelve." She eyed me curiously. "I'm glad you came. I deal only with Luanne, so I never would have gotten a call from the publisher or the agent. I don't even think they know about me. If you hadn't told me, I would have been calling and leaving messages on her phone. Last time I spoke with her, it was Friday night and she was still planning to come by today. What with our internet down, and I don't read the papers or watch much television besides the kids' shows… I get so caught up with getting dinner on the table and the kids. Judah's got a science fair project due, and Rachel's recital is coming up, and Hannah won't sleep a wink unless I read to her every night. I might not have found out for weeks. Poor thing."

"So, you ghostwrite for her?" Daisy asked. "And neither the agent or the publisher knows about it? They think Fanged Darkness is actually written by Luanne?"

She nodded. "I guess the cat's out of the bag with her being gone and all—God rest her soul. Shame. It was fun writing those books, and easy working for Luanne. Well, except for that Barton Wells thing. I almost refused to write any more for her after that."

"The publisher didn't know? Eva, her agent, didn't know?" I asked, just to confirm. "No one knew besides Luanne?"

Her laugh was downright charming, the dimples back in her cheeks. "Oh, heavens no! I mean, my husband knows, of course, and my sister, but that's it. Luanne bought my books directly from me. Part of our agreement was that no one would know I wrote them."

If no one knew…I frowned, wondering about the assistant producer and the legal issue Eva had hinted about. Clearly the cat had been out of the bag before last night. And hadn't Eva said that the series would be finished, and even a third series published?

"Book seven is about to be released and I saw the manuscript for book eight in Luanne's briefcase. Do you have the other books written already and submitted to Luanne? And another spin-off series?"

She shook her head. "No. I guess that's over now that she's gone. Oh, I'll probably write the last two books in the series because I have to finish things out, you know. But it's not like they'll ever be published with Luanne passed on."

"Can I read them?" Daisy hurriedly asked. "Unedited. On

notebook paper. Scraps of napkins. I don't care. I just want to read the last two books in the series."

Gerry shot her an odd look. "I guess, if you promise not to tell anyone about them. It might be a while, though. With Luanne gone, it's not like I have deadlines or anything."

"Wait." I frowned, trying to puzzle this out. "You've known Luanne for twelve years. And you've been writing for her for ten? That's when the first Infernal Awakenings book was published, right? And that's one of yours."

Gerry nodded. "I actually wrote that ages ago. Luanne bought that series, then it took a few years for Luanne to sell them, and another three years for the publishing company to release them. There was a lot of delay at first, but once things started moving, Luanne was needing two or three books a year from me. It was so exciting."

"Twelve years," Daisy commented. "What were you, ten when you wrote that? You don't look a day over twenty-two."

Dimples creased the woman's cheeks once more. "Oh, thank you, hon! I'm thirty, but it's so nice to hear that. I wrote the first Infernal Awakenings book when I was sixteen but didn't get up the nerve to show it to anyone until I was eighteen. I'd always been writing things, ever since I was a little girl. Mostly they were stories about dogs and little kids and Jesus and stuff, but when I got into high school..." She blushed becomingly. "Let's just say I started reading things my mama wouldn't have called wholesome. And my writing went that direction. I hid it all under my mattress, not sure whether I should burn it before my parents found it or not."

"How did you meet Luanne?" What I meant was how in the world did she go from scribbling in notebooks to writing some of the bestselling romance novels of the last ten years?

"There was one of those book conventions in Richmond. I was engaged and hoping to see if maybe I could sell my books to help us get started in our own house. John encouraged me to go and talk to the agents there. Of course, I was thinking I was going to sell some of my children's religious stories, not the racy ones. I still have no idea why I put that manuscript in my bag that day."

"John?" I glanced up at the gigantic crucifix.

"My husband, Reverend John Pook, although we were just engaged at the time. He'd read my stuff and thought it was really good. All my stuff, because when you're marrying, you shouldn't have secrets from each other, not even the smut under the bed."

Daisy made a strangled sound. "No, the smut under the bed should definitely not be a secret from your husband."

Gerry laughed, the sound light and musical. "John never had any problem with smut under the bed, but those stories are not the kind of stuff a preacher's wife who teaches Sunday school should be publishing. Originally, I was going to sell the children's stuff, but nobody wanted them."

"So, you broke out the Infernal Awakenings book and figured you'd give it a go?" I asked.

She nodded. "I met Luanne in one of those panel discussion things. She was so smart, knew how things worked in those New York publishing houses and all that, so I showed her the story and asked what she thought. A few days later, she calls me up and tells me she'll buy everything I write. Everything."

"Everything except the kids' religious stories," Daisy said with an arched eyebrow.

"Sadly, yes. Maybe someday I'll be able to sell those. In the meantime, I use them in our Sunday school classes."

"And your husband was on board with this?" I asked, thinking smut under the bed was a whole lot different than smut out on the front table of a bookstore.

"Oh, yes, as long as they used someone else's name and I didn't have to go to signings or have my picture on the internet where someone might recognize me. He and I both figured it would be okay if someone just bought the stories and published them under their own name and nobody ever knew I wrote them."

So this deal with Luanne seemed perfect on both of their ends. It sounded straightforward to me. No need for Geraldine to drive to Milford and crack Luanne Trainor upside the head. If it had been murder and not an accident, that is.

"You were happy with the money she was paying you?" I asked, just to be sure.

"Oh, yes. The contract says I'm supposed to get a thousand dollars per book, but the last few years Luanne's been sending me two thousand. It's a nice little extra for the kids' college funds, you know?" She clapped her hands over her cheeks. "Oh, no! I was so excited to hear the rumors that there would be a movie made. Do you think they'll still do it with Luanne gone? Imagine sitting in a theater and watching something you wrote up on the screen, and nobody knows it was you." Her smile was mischievous.

I could see how this would be an ideal arrangement for her. None of her husband's parishioners or the parents of the kids she taught would find out that sweet Gerry Pook wrote that kinky stuff with vampires and demons. She seemed happy with the situation. I felt a little uncomfortable with the idea that she was getting one or two thousand per book while Luanne Trainor got one or two hundred thousand per book, but maybe the success was due in part to the author's already-established name. Maybe Luanne Trainor had worked her butt off to make sure those books sold. Either way, it was clear that Gerry Pook had nothing to do with Luanne's death. If anything, the woman would lose a couple thousand extra per year because of it.

"They announced the film deal last night," Daisy told her. "So I'm assuming it's still a go. I mean, the publishing company owns the film rights, and the books are already written, so it shouldn't be a problem."

Gerry frowned. "Oh, the paperwork. I wonder if they still need it? Luanne sent me a new contract a few weeks ago that I was supposed to sign and get back to her, but with everything going on and no internet and my printer down... She ended up overnighting me a hard copy on Thursday and said she'd be by this morning to pick it up, but I didn't have time to get to a notary."

"Maybe Luanne would have just forged a notary," Daisy whispered to me with a roll of her eyes. I was pretty sure she wasn't wrong.

And I was pretty sure Eva was going to need those papers. I suspected that someone at the film company had gotten wind of Geraldine's involvement and wanted all their bases covered before they started production—hence the scowling Sebastian at the theater and Eva's vague comments about a legal issue.

"I'm sure Luanne's agent and her publisher would want that contract," I told Gerry. "Is there a way you can get it notarized tomorrow? I'll give you her agent's address and maybe you can mail it to her, or she can swing by and pick it up. I remember her saying she wouldn't be going back to New York for a few days yet."

Gerry rooted around on the table and grabbed a coloring book and a green crayon to write down Eva's name and number. "Thank you so much! I'll definitely get that notarized and in the mail to her. Did you want a copy of the contract? To take to her in case she wants any modifications before I drive around to find a notary? I don't have a fax or internet so maybe you can give it to her tonight or tomorrow?"

Nosy me. My heart leapt at the chance. "That would be

great. Maybe both contracts so Eva can see what you and Luanne had originally agreed to and the changes?"

"Sure." Gerry stood. "My printer is dead, though, so I can't make copies. Can you just take pictures of them with your cell phone and send them to the agent that way?"

The woman vanished down a hallway without waiting for my response and Daisy leaned over to me. "No internet. Broken printer. And she clearly doesn't have a smartphone herself. Heck, I doubt she even has a flip phone. Have we been transported back into 1980? Are they Luddites?"

I shushed her. "I think she's just busy and all that's not a priority. She's probably got a million church things to do, and I swear I hear a dozen kids down in that basement with the television."

Daisy giggled. "A dozen kids in a dozen years of marriage. I'd say the woman who wrote all that steamy stuff has been acting out all that stuff between the pages."

"Well, she did say her husband knew and approved of the smut under the bed."

We both laughed, then tried to compose ourselves as Gerry dashed back into the room, papers in hand.

I snapped pictures of each contract, then we all settled in for another iced tea and zucchini bread while Daisy and I asked a million questions to the creative mind behind the two bestselling series. A crash and a loud voice in the basement along with a harried look from Geraldine signaled that we'd reached the end of our visit. With pleasant goodbyes and promises to keep in touch, Daisy and I left the woman kissing a boo-boo and arbitrating some dispute between what did seem like a dozen children who'd trooped up from the basement.

Back in the car, Daisy sighed and leaned back against the headrest. "Okay, now I'm glad I don't have kids. Whew, that place was a tornado of toys and noise."

"If you'd had kids, you'd be used to it," I told her. "And Gerry seems pretty happy with it all."

"She does." Daisy smiled and grabbed my phone from the console. "You know, she's nice. And she *is* a good salesperson. I've never been so close to converting in my life."

I laughed. "It's the zucchini bread. No one can resist its siren call. Baked goods are probably responsible for sixty percent of church membership."

"True." Daisy held up my phone. "Do you mind? I want to eyeball those contracts she brought out."

I nodded, pulling out of Gerry's driveway and down the street. Might as well. I was beginning to feel a bit uncomfortable with my level of nosiness today, but in for a penny, in for a pound.

CHAPTER 15

"Get out."

Daisy turned to me, her brows raised. "Me? Because you're going sixty-five on the highway right now. I'd rather not 'get out' if it's okay with you."

"Not you." I jerked my head toward the back seat, glancing through the rearview.

Daisy spun around, eyeballed the back seat, then shot me a perplexed look.

"Holt. Or rather Holt's ghost," I told her. The spirit hadn't shown up during yoga in spite of Daisy insisting that Luanne's death was a murder, so I'd assumed the ghost had taken my warning to heart last night and was staying away until Monday. I'd clearly assumed wrong because there was now a dark shadow in the back of my sedan. As I watched, the seatbelt pulled across and clicked safely into place.

"Whoa!" Daisy exclaimed, wide-eyed.

"My driving isn't that bad," I told the ghost. "Besides, you're dead already."

"Well, *I'm* not dead, so keep your eyes on the road," Daisy scolded. "Has he been showing up like this? I thought once their murderer was ousted, they floated off to heaven or something. Or at the very least, went somewhere else and left you alone. Well, except for Eli, that is."

"He's sticking around." I told Daisy about the conversation with the spirit through Olive. "Seems he wants to be a ghost detective. We made a deal that he wouldn't bother me unless I was working. He's clearly violating that agreement because I'm not working. Luanne's death was an *accident*." I glared into the rearview for a quick second to emphasize the last sentence.

"Yeah, but you are kind of sleuthing here," Daisy pointed out. "Investigating the details of the ghostwriting arrangement between Gerry and Luanne and figuring out who really wrote Infernal Awakenings and Fanged Darkness. So in a way, it sort of is detective work."

"Whose side are you on?" I scowled at my friend.

"Just ignore him," Daisy advised. "Unless he starts trashing the car, just ignore him."

"Easy for you to say. You can't see him."

She laughed. "Yeah, well if you stop looking in the rearview, you wouldn't be able to see him, either. Let's check out these contracts instead. What's your phone password?"

I told her and waited while Daisy read, trying my hardest not to look in the rearview at the ghost in my back seat. Finally, my friend looked up with a sigh and shook her head.

"I'm wishing I was a lawyer right now, because I'm pretty sure that poor woman has been taken to the cleaners."

"She seemed happy with the deal," I reminded Daisy. "In fact, she seemed thrilled. It's not our place to say. Those books would have been a stack of papers shoved under a bed if Luanne hadn't bought them. And I'm sure Luanne contributed a lot to the marketing success, if not the actual content."

"No amount of marketing would have made those books

bestsellers if they hadn't been written the way they were," Daisy argued. "What Luanne did was predatory. She conned a young, inexperienced writer out of her work, paying her a pittance while she rolled in the bucks. It's wrong."

I glanced in the rearview and let out a breath when I realized Holt had vanished. I guess our conversation hadn't kept his attention. Either that or the homeless on South Street had something really interesting going on right now.

"It is wrong," I agreed, tired of defending a woman I hadn't liked at all. "Gerry is a babe in the woods. She probably didn't know how well those books were selling. If she had, I'm not sure she would have continued to write for Luanne once the Infernal Awakenings series was over. At least not for what Luanne was paying her for as an unknown author." Although I wasn't sure about that. Luanne had doubled the money she'd originally been giving Gerry. And although I felt the deal was very lopsided, Gerry had seemed to not take issue with it. Maybe the anonymity of it all was worth the extra money to her. Maybe it was worth it just to know her books had been published and read, and that she'd been able to add to the kids' college funds.

"Have you seen this contract?" Daisy had my phone in hand, scrolling through the picture I'd taken. "I've seen better deals in crayon on a diner napkin."

"It's that bad?"

"You should run it by Judge Beck when you get home." She set the phone down. "Speaking of which, where was he this morning? I'm used to seeing him wandering around the kitchen in his pajamas with his hair all mussed up. I miss that. It kinda makes my day, you know?"

"Insomnia. He was up when I got home, drinking tea. He was still up when I finally went off to bed, so I'm assuming he slept in. Then he probably went out to golf whenever he rolled out of bed. That's pretty much what he does on the weekends that he doesn't have the kids."

"Bet that's part of his insomnia." Daisy gave me a knowing nod. "Dad always told me he slept better when his kids were all under one roof. Of course, I was forty when he told me that, but I guess kids are always kids to their parents."

"That and I think the divorce has hit a rocky patch," I confessed. "He lets things slip sometimes, and my heart just hurts for him."

"That divorce has been in a rocky patch since day one." Daisy patted my hand on the steering wheel. "I'm glad you're there for him to talk to. Imagine how horrible it would be for him living in some sterile apartment, all alone except for when the kids were there."

"It's not all one-sided," I confessed. "I love having him around. Taco is amazing, but it was nice to come home last night and find him in the kitchen with the kettle on."

"In his pajamas? With his hair all mussed?" Daisy teased. "Seriously though, I hope the divorce wraps up soon. Poor guy. I'm sure Heather is going to take him for every penny he's got."

"He'd be happy to give her every penny he had if he could have the kids full time," I told her. "He knows they need to see their mother, but he worries she'll do something to deny him half custody. I know he'd really like full custody, though."

Daisy shot me a perceptive glance. "Think that's a possibility?"

"No. And that's not necessarily a bad thing. Full custody would pretty much end his career. His heart wants his children at home every night, but in reality, without a wife to do all the after-school pick up and drop off, he'd never be able to get his work done. He manages now by working double-time in the weeks he doesn't have the kids." I shook my head sadly. "I admire him for making it work, but I worry he's pushing himself too hard."

"Maybe they'll get back together." Daisy's comment was a shade too casual. I glared at her.

"Heather has a boyfriend. And although Judge Beck is clearly not over the break-up of his marriage, I think he feels things are too far gone at this point to salvage the relationship."

"Just saying that as things get tough, as things get down to the wire, there may be an attempt at reconciliation. That boyfriend thing might be short-lived, and all sorts of memories about how things used to be might lead them to give it another try." Daisy patted my hand again. "I don't want you to be hurt."

"Too late," I told her. "I'd miss the kids terribly. I'd miss the judge terribly. Although I know that even if they don't get back together, once this is all final he'll buy a home of his own and move out. My only hope is that the kids will want to see me after that—to spend time with me every now and then and maybe write me, or e-mail me, from college."

"And Judge Beck?" Daisy's voice was soft.

"He's my friend. He's like family to me. But the reality is that once this divorce is final, he'll start dating and eventually find someone and fall in love." I took a deep breath. "I don't harbor any hopes that he'll bother to keep in touch with me after that. Maybe a Christmas card, or something, but that's it."

"Oh, Kay..."

"That's the way it goes," I told her, marveling at how my voice was steady and strong. "Honestly, it might be for the best. He's been such a comfort to me after Eli's passing, but in a year or so, once he's gone, I'll need to start learning to live alone. I need to learn to be happy with my friends and with Taco, and not rely on having someone there every night when I come home."

"If you're not dating by then, I'm going to start setting you up," Daisy insisted. "You're too young to be single the rest of your life. Eli wouldn't have wanted that. You need to date. And maybe you'll find another man to love and marry."

"So says the woman who has been single her entire life." I was teasing, but a quick glance at my friend made me realize my words had hurt her. "Oh, Daisy. I didn't mean that…"

She gave me a wan smile. "It's okay. It's not by choice, you know. I mean, maybe it's by choice, but I never stopped hoping I'd find the right guy. I dated a lot when I was younger. Was engaged once. Sometimes you learn to be happy alone because that's what life has dealt you."

"And this is what life has dealt me," I told her softly. "I loved Eli. Even after the accident with how much he'd changed, I loved him. I don't think I have it in me to love like that again. And I'm worried that if I open myself up, anything I do will be some sort of rebound. A man doesn't deserve to be my second choice, my Band-Aid for a love lost. A man deserves a hundred percent of me, not some fake love based on loneliness and grief."

"I think you do have it in you, Kay." She turned in her seat to face me. "Those kids will eventually grow up and get lives of their own. Judge Beck…well, who knows what Judge Beck will do? You've got your friends. You've got Taco. And I know you think that's enough, but I don't want you to let an opportunity pass you by because you won't open yourself to the thought that you could love more than one person in your life."

I thought of my future, of my elderly years. There were so many people I knew like Matt's father, who were widowed with only the few friends still alive and occasional visits from their children for company. I wasn't anywhere near that part of my life yet. "Okay, I promise I'll open my mind and heart to the possibility, but only if you do the same." I wagged a finger at her.

She leaned back in her seat. "I know. I know. I should probably go out with J.T. He's asked often enough."

I shrugged. "If you can't bear the thought of suffering through a plate of linguini with him, then don't. He's a nice guy. He's smart and gets along with everyone he meets. Plus, that reality show thing is just enough quirky silliness to make him interesting."

"He's also pretty good at wrestling gun-toting, homicidal mayors to the ground," Daisy added. "And he's kinda cute with the shaved head and cowboy boot look he's got going on lately."

"Then why do you keep turning him down? He's not going to keep asking forever, you know. Even J.T. has a limit to his persistence."

She wrinkled her nose in thought. "He's slick. He's a bit of a smooth talker who's buddies with all the guys and a flirt with all the ladies. I've been burned by that kind of guy before."

"J.T.'s flirting never crosses the line, and he's not the kind that dates around. I think he really likes you, Daisy. And you've known him since high school, haven't you?"

She sniffed. "He was a flirt back then, too. I don't know. I just never really thought of J.T. Pierson as someone I'd go out with. He never really hit my radar as a guy I wanted to date."

"Sometimes love isn't a lightning bolt, it's a slow incoming tide that catches you by surprise. And it's just dinner. It's not like he's going to stuff you in a car and drive to Atlantic City for a shotgun wedding."

She chuckled, then grew serious once more. "Was it a slow incoming tide with Eli?"

"No. Eli was a lightning bolt. But he wasn't the unobtainable football player I'd always drooled over either. He was a skinny Latino guy who had three hundred pounds of books in his backpack and a cup of coffee permanently attached to one hand. But there was this gentle humor about him and when he looked at me, when he talked to me, his full attention was on *me*—not the next day's chemistry exam, or what party was going on this weekend, or if he had enough money to chip in for pizza night. Me. That sort of thing is sexy. It's intoxicating. I was in love from the moment I met him."

I glanced over at Daisy and saw the shadow of longing in her eyes.

"Okay. You win," She raised her hands in surrender. "I'll call J.T. as soon as we get home. I'm not promising anything, but I'll give the guy a chance."

I hid a smile. "And I swear that when I'm ready, when I feel like my heart has healed enough to let another in, I'll give someone a chance."

Daisy shot me a sideways glance. "Promise?"

I took one hand off the wheel to raise it. "Promise."

CHAPTER 16

"This is a mess." Judge Beck handed me back my phone. "It's been a while since I've done contract law, but it's my learned opinion that whoever wrote that thing up should be taken out back and whipped."

I looked down at my phone. "That bad?"

He sighed. "Verbal contracts are binding, and most judges like to err on the side of intent when it comes to things like this, but..."

"Could Gerry have gone after Luanne for more money if she'd wanted to? Or the publisher?"

"Probably. That contract is so vague that any lawsuit would wind up being a she-said-she-said. And in that case, without any witnesses or notaries to state what the original agreed-upon intent was, the judge would look at what a reasonable person would have considered fair under those circumstances, and rule that way."

"Meaning?"

"It looks like one book was contracted for a fee of one thousand dollars. I know it doesn't seem fair since that Trainor woman was probably making a ten-thousand-dollar advance plus royalties, but that was what was agreed upon. There was no obligation for Mrs. Pook to continue writing for that amount past the first book. The fact that she did would tell me she was satisfied with the terms, no matter how lopsided they seemed. Even I have seen those vampire romance books prominently displayed on the front tables at bookstores. Mrs. Pook had to have realized that Ms. Trainor was making far more than she was, but she never requested additional compensation for the other books beyond what this contract says."

"But audio, film, and foreign rights?"

"That's where it gets tricky—and where I'm a bit out of my area of expertise. The way I'm reading this, I'd interpret the contract to mean only e-book and print rights are conveyed. It doesn't specify whether those rights include translated works, but I'd be inclined to rule that the general nature of the contract does include translations. Film and audio...those formats aren't addressed at all in the original contract, so I would rule they are not included. But contract lawyers who specialize in intellectual property or creative works might have a different take on it."

I mulled over his words. "I'm wondering how paranoid production companies are when they buy the film rights to something. I can see an audio firm taking the word of a big-name publishing company that they own all the rights, but would a producer dig a little deeper? And if they found out there was a ghostwriter who wasn't mentioned in the deal, wouldn't they want to see the contract between the ghost-writer and the publisher? And if the publisher had no idea about the ghostwriter..."

"Then the film company would probably be very hesitant about the deal until all the details were locked in on paper. There's a whole lot more at stake with movies. Audio production is, what, three or four thousand per book?

Producing a film costs millions. And you said the author had already been hit with a plagiarism suit? That's going to make a company offering to buy the film rights doubly nervous."

"From what the agent said, the plagiarism suit was dismissed. Summary judgment, or something like that."

"Still, it might have made the producer want their attorney to look at the contract between the publishing company and Ms. Trainor to double check any possibility of collaborators or ghostwriters, and to clarify who indemnifies who in case of a lawsuit."

"I can't imagine how they found out about Gerry though," I mused, "even with the plagiarism suit. I got the impression that the agreement was all hush-hush between Luanne and Gerry. Gerry said that the publishing company, even Luanne's agent, didn't know those books were ghostwritten. That no one beyond Luanne, her husband, and her sister knew."

"The husband was having a beer in a bar and started bragging?" the judge suggested.

I shot him a sideways look. "The guy is a minister."

"Ministers drink. And ministers have been known to brag about their talented wives as well."

"Talented wives who write about explicit sexual relationships between women and demons? Or vampires?"

He grimaced. "Okay, maybe not."

"The contract between Luanne and the publisher would have looked boilerplate, and no one would have ever known about Gerry's involvement, let alone questioned whether she'd conveyed the film rights in her deal with Luanne. How did they find out? How did anyone find out?"

"They had to have found out somehow." The judge pointed at my phone. "The other contract, the one Gerry hadn't gotten around to signing yet, is professionally done and does include all formats and specifically notes the film rights. If I had to hazard a guess, I'd assume Ms. Trainor modeled it after the ones she signs with the publishing company. I'm going to assume that the news leaked out. Ms. Trainor got wind of it and was trying to dot all the legal 'i's before either the film deal went belly up or the publisher accused her of breach of contract and sued her for damages."

I frowned. "Could they do that? Breach of contract? Really?"

"I'm pretty sure her contract with the publisher included an assertion that these works were her own and that she owned all the rights to them. So yes, breach of contract. I doubt they would have tossed her to the curb with her name on all those bestsellers, but they'd definitely have significant leverage over her in future contract negotiations. They could threaten to expose the deal, go straight to Gerry for the books, and strip Ms. Trainor's name from the novels. She'd go down in disgrace."

I caught my breath. Luanne's own books hadn't been all that great. Without Gerry writing for her, she'd be nothing. And after everything went public, she'd be blacklisted. He was right. I would have felt sorry for Luanne had she not been such a horrible, nasty human being.

"If Gerry had signed the new contract, would it have been legal?" I asked. "I mean, she'd be giving away additional rights without any additional compensation. Doesn't that void the contract?"

"It would have been legal. Unless she was drugged or drunk or somehow forced to sign it, it would have been legal. Sometimes contracts are revised and no additional compensation is given. I've seen it happen when a previous contract is vague or there are situations the parties assumed but weren't addressed in writing."

"She was going to sign it," I told him. "She just had to find time to go to some office place to make copies because her printer was broken. Then she needed to go to the bank and have it notarized before sending it in. Luanne was pushing her to hurry, but the woman has like a dozen kids and is really busy with her husband's church. Even if Luanne had convinced me to detour there on the way to dropping her off at the airport, Gerry wouldn't have had it notarized yet. And it's Sunday. I don't think there's anywhere to get something notarized on a Sunday."

"If Ms. Trainor had a signed contract showing that she owned all rights, then it probably would have blown over. The publisher would have slapped her on the wrist for not letting them know, but I'm guessing as long as the lawyers felt the contract looked solid, the film deal would have gone through and all would have been okay."

"But it was all going to blow up before she could get the new contract," I mused. "And the old one was so horrible that the film company would have run away, taking their offer with them. Luanne had to have that new contract—and she had to have it yesterday."

"Well, now that she's dead, it's kind of a moot point, isn't it? So what is the ghostwriter going to do?" Judge Beck motioned again toward my phone. "Gerry. I guess she can get it notarized and send it to the agent. Ms. Trainor's death shouldn't hold up the film production or the final contracted books as long as your ghostwriter is amenable. It wouldn't be the first time books have been published posthumously. It doesn't sound like Gerry wants her name on any of the books, so future novels would just continue to be released as Luanne Trainor books and everything would proceed business-as-usual."

I shrugged. "I left a message over at the inn for Eva to call me. I'll text these over to her once I get her cell phone and I'm assuming she'll contact Gerry and have her sign with the agency and with the publishing company. Eva will probably want to make sure the last few books in the series are firmed up with her as well as the film rights. And I think there was talk of a third series, too."

I guessed Gerry *would* be happy to continue seeing those books published posthumously under Luanne's name. Judge Beck was right—it wasn't unheard of. I'd read of a crime fiction author who'd been publishing for ten years past his death through ghostwriters contracted through his estate. As long as the writing was as good—which it would be—none of the readers would really care. At the end of the day, they only wanted an engaging story with their favorite characters, no matter who was putting words to paper behind the scenes.

Yes, Gerry was getting ripped off, but she didn't seem to care. The woman was thrilled that no one in her husband's church or any of her family beyond her sister knew about her hobby. She was equally thrilled to be making some spare money off her work. She wrote at her own pace. Outside of Barton Wells, she had complete creative control. And that money had added up over the years to quite a nice supplemental income in her eyes. There were ten Infernal Awakenings books and six Fanged Darkness books to date. That was anywhere from sixteen to thirty-two thousand dollars she'd made depending on when Luanne had started paying her extra. And in spite of the millions everyone else had made from the books, Gerry was obviously satisfied with what she'd received.

Neither she nor her husband seemed resentful. Neither would have wanted Luanne Trainor dead. If the author hadn't died, everything would have gone on as before. Luanne's death hadn't really changed anything for Gerry. As far as murder suspects went, I felt safe ruling out Gerry and her husband.

Not that there was a murder. Although with Daisy's continued insistence, I'd begun to wonder if Luanne's death wasn't an accident after all, even though there was nothing from what I could see at the parking garage to lead me to believe otherwise.

Accident or not? I'd ask J.T. tomorrow at work. He knew all the police and was probably on a first-name basis with all the people at the medical examiner's office. If there was the slightest hint of foul play, my boss would know. And maybe then I could put my curiosity and my suspicions to rest.

CHAPTER 17

I got up early on Monday and made maple spice scones as well as my favorite cherry vanilla ones—a double batch of each so I'd have enough to take in to work. I'd gotten to the office, had a pot of coffee brewing, and was thumbing through the skip-trace files when Holt appeared, a dark indistinct shape over near the copy machine.

"We've got an exciting day today," I told the ghost. "Two people with bad debts to track down and a car repossession. We won't actually be repossessing the car, just figuring out where the guy has it stashed. Pretty much the whole day is going to be me doing searches on the computer and typing up reports." I figured one day of watching me do the most boring detective work ever would send Holt right to the afterlife. Personally, I found the research interesting, but I doubted the ghost of a young football player would. He probably thought I was going to be chasing down criminals and tackling drug dealers in back alleys like in the movies. Boy, was he about to get a surprise.

I'd just sat down with my cup of coffee and began sorting

through one of the files when J.T. came waltzing in, making a beeline for the scones.

Waltzing. More like skipping. The man was downright giddy with excitement.

"Have a good weekend?" I asked.

"Actually yes. Better than yours, I hear."

I grimaced. "This is becoming a habit of mine, finding the recently deceased. It's a habit I'm not particularly thrilled about."

"From what Nancy told me, no one is going to be crying at her funeral." J.T. poured himself a cup of coffee then turned to sit on the edge of the table. "Unless she left a series hanging, that is. No one likes an unfinished series."

Huh. He was friends with Nancy? Friends enough that he'd gotten the details of the disastrous event the day afterward? I made a mental note never to doubt J.T.'s information network.

"I can pretty much guarantee there won't be any unfinished series, even for decades to come," I drawled. "She certainly wasn't a very nice person, and both Nancy and Paula Billingsly probably got the worst of her terrible social skills, but I still wouldn't want the woman dead."

"You talking about that author woman?" Miles walked through the door, sighted the scones, and went straight for them.

"Word certainly travels fast," I told him.

"Well, you know, two celebrity deaths within two months." Miles bit into the pastry. "It's gotta be a record or something."

The officer and I had struck up a sort-of friendship during the Holt Dupree investigation, and now he was a regular at the offices of Pierson Investigative and Recovery Services—especially on Mondays when I tended to bring in home-baked goods.

"I was first on the scene for both those celebrity deaths," I reminded him. "It was a bit of a shock finding Luanne Trainor sprawled at the bottom of the steps leading out of the parking garage."

"She was at the exit heading out into that little street behind the taco place, wasn't she? There's only three steps up to the door at that exit. What did she do, slip on a banana peel or something?"

I shrugged. "That's for you guys to determine, not me."

Miles' phone buzzed and he looked down at it before stuffing the rest of the scone in his mouth and stepping into the back office to answer the call. Holt's ghost moved from the copier to stand in front of the doorway. Miles shivered as he passed through the spirit, and I noticed Holt followed the officer in a drifting fog sort of way.

I sipped my coffee and looked through my work for the day. J.T. had filled out the paperwork for me to get my actual license, but even after I was authorized to do actual detective work, I'd still be primarily responsible for the online investigative side of the business. Although being a licensed PI wouldn't change my duties all that much, it still thrilled me that I'd soon have a slip of paper and new business cards, making it all official.

Journalist. Then caretaker and freelance writer. Then skip tracer and soon-to-be detective. This job had started out as a way to make ends meet and put food on the table, but I was loving my new career.

"Oh, and thanks by the way. I owe you one." J.T. grabbed another scone and waved it at me.

I raised my eyebrows and gave him a puzzled look.

"I have a date tonight," he told me with a smug smile.

"Daisy?"

"Finally. I guess I have you to thank for that."

"Just make sure you run a razor over your head and wear your cowboy boots," I told him. "Where are you two going?"

"Manzana's downtown. You can't go wrong with pasta, and they've got the whole dim-room, candlelight and chianti atmosphere down pat."

"Don't get too romantic," I warned him. "Daisy wants interesting conversation more than smarmy compliments. I mean, a few compliments are always welcome, but don't go overboard, okay?"

He nodded. "Any topics I should avoid?"

I laughed. "Depends on how spirited you want the conversation. Get her talking about her work, or community events, or local history. You guys grew up together. Surely you've got a lot of past in common you can discuss?"

"We both knew each other, but we didn't hang in the same social circles when we were kids. Or as adults, either. Honestly, I hadn't seen Daisy in years until you started working for me."

"You'll do fine," I assured him, hoping it was the truth. Yes, my boss was quirky, but so was my best friend. I didn't want to force a square peg into a round hole, but if the pair of them hit it off, I'd be thrilled.

"Guys!" Miles burst back into the room, waving his phone in excitement, Holt's ghostly shadow so close behind him that he actually did look like Miles' shadow. "I just got off the phone with my buddy over in Milford. He just got the Luanne Trainor case on his board!"

J.T. and I exchanged perplexed looks. "Case?"

"Murder." Miles nodded smugly. "The M.E.'s office rushed it since she was a celebrity and the brother is pushing to have the body shipped out to Chicago. Seems someone bashed her on the back of the head."

I stared at him. "Why didn't anyone notice that at the scene? Paramedics? The police? And what in the heck did they hit her with that broke her neck, because although her head was…" I shuddered. "Well, I'm no doctor and I could tell her neck was broken."

"No, someone hit her on the back of the head, then she fell forward and whacked the front part of her head on the edge of the step. Everyone assumed the blood was from the side of her face. Plus, with all that poofy red hair, nobody saw the wound on the back of her head until the M.E. got a look at her."

I frowned, visualizing the scene. "But there was no weapon. I didn't see anything there that an attacker could have used to hit her with."

"Maybe he took it with him," Miles suggested. "Or stashed it in a parked car."

J.T. snorted. "Milford isn't exactly crime central, but no one leaves their car unlocked, especially in a parking garage. The guy either took the weapon with him or stashed it somewhere."

Miles nodded. "If everyone assumed it was an accident, no one would have been searching the parking garage for a weapon. He could have just tossed it in the stairwell or out into the back dumpster and no one would have known."

I shook my head in disbelief. So Daisy was right. Luanne's death *wasn't* an accident after all. "So someone pushed her." I mused. "No, not pushed her. Someone hit her. Was the blow to the head severe enough to prove intent to kill?"

Miles shrugged. "That's for the lawyers to decide. It was certainly severe enough to cause injury and make her fall to her death. Plus, whoever did it must have seen her fall. They left her there, dead on the parking garage floor."

He was right. An innocent person would have called for help, not snuck off and left poor Luanne there for me to find. Well, not *poor* Luanne, but still the woman didn't deserve to be murdered.

"Your friend has the case?" I asked Miles, immediately wondering how I could somehow weasel myself into the investigation. If it were Miles, I would have no problem, but a detective I didn't know in Milford, and me without an official P.I.'s license yet...

"Desmond Keeler," he told me. "And he wants to see you as soon as possible. Since you found the body and had helped with the event, you know."

I grinned, ready to grab my purse and drive straight to Milford. Holt's ghost did the same. Well, except without the purse. I eyed the shadow, thinking that today was turning out to be a lot more exciting than skip traces and repossession research.

"When am I supposed to meet the detective?" I asked Miles.

"I told him you'd just gotten in and to give you until around eleven." Miles turned to J.T. "Is that okay? I'm sure Kay has work to do, but..."

My boss puffed his chest out. "Consulting on a major case like this? Of course it's okay. We're happy to be a resource to the Milford P.D."

"Well, it's not exactly as a consultant. She was there on the scene. He needs to interview her. It's not like Kay is going to be working on the case with him."

J.T. grinned. "Of course she will. I have every confidence that five minutes after meeting Kay, she'll be consulting on the case. Free of charge, of course. We want to show the Milford P.D. how valuable a resource our firm is so they continue to use us in future cases. I'll contact their accounts payable department and start the paperwork for billing and contracts, just like I've done with the Locust Point P.D. and the county sheriff's office."

Miles put his hands up, a half-eaten scone still in one of them. "I'm not guaranteeing anything, J.T., especially with the

Milford guys. It's up to Keeler if he wants to take you up on the offer or not."

I looked from the officer to the container of scones by the coffee maker and smiled, knowing I had the perfect bribe for Detective Desmond Keeler. Perfect.

CHAPTER 18

"So..." The detective eyed the container of scones. "Miles told me I should interview you sooner rather than later. He said you're some kinda Miss Marple, or something?"

I smiled over at the man, trying to ignore the shadow lurking behind him. Holt had followed me from my office to the Milford police station. I'd made him ride in the back.

"If I were Miss Marple, we'd have a confessed killer in custody and you and I would be sitting here drinking tea, eating those little sandwiches with the crusts cut off and discussing the weather." He eyed the scones again and I pushed them forward a few inches. "Instead, let's talk crime scene and suspects and have coffee and scones."

"You make those?" His desire for the pastries was palpable.

"Yes, I did."

"And you work for Pierson, right?"

"Yes." Technically I was still a skip tracer until the paperwork came in to make me a licensed investigator, but J.T. had given this visit his enthusiastic blessing. The more we coordinated with local and neighboring police, the easier our job would be. And from what he'd said in the office this morning, he had some idea of consulting work with the local officers. Which sounded good to me. I'd love it if my job included this sort of thing. Well, maybe not with murder, though.

"Pierson gave us some tips a few years back on that string of break-ins. Heard he solved the case with your mayor, too. And the one with the football player."

It was me that had done the latter two, but I was happy to let the agency take the credit. "I'm sure Miles told you how helpful we were coordinating with police on the Holt Dupree murder."

He nodded, eyes still fixed on the scones. "That's why you're sitting here instead of me just using the statement you gave at the scene."

Right. I took the lid off the container and extended the box of scones toward him. "Cherry vanilla and maple spice."

The man took one and bit into it. I swear his eyes nearly rolled backward in his head. "So," he said, his mouth full of scone. "Tell me exactly what happened leading up to your finding the body."

I went over my search for Luanne, leaving out the ghost, and ending with my discovery of the author at the foot of the steps.

"So then I called 911 and waited there for the police to show up."

"Hmmm." He reached in the box for another scone and set the paper down. "So, you were following her around since you picked her up at the airport Friday morning, right?"

"Not really. I picked her up at the airport, dropped her at the B&B, then didn't see her again until the next morning for the brunch. Then I went home to get some things ready and came back about an hour before we were due at the theater. I was with her pretty much from that point until I found her—well, except for when she pulled her disappearing act at the meet-and-greet and I had to go look for her."

He nodded. "So, let's hear it. Who do you think would have wanted Luanne Trainor dead?"

I snorted. "It's more like who *wouldn't* have wanted her dead. We've got the obvious suspects—those fans upset about the death of Barton Wells, for starters. Eva said they'd been sending nasty letters to Luanne and even a cow's heart. It came up at the brunch, and one of the attendees came back later and fought with Luanne, according to Gene and Paula. Her name is Amy Shep."

The detective blinked a few times. "Gene and Paula, the B&B owners, right? They witnessed this...argument? Brawl? And Eva is the agent woman? But who is Barton Wells and what is this about him dying and some cow's heart?"

"Barton Wells was a character in the books." I waved my hand in the air. "It doesn't matter except that quite a lot of Luanne's fans evidently went bonkers when she killed him off and she got threats. And a cow's heart. Twice. Once last year in the mail and then the one this Amy Shep brought."

He nodded, a bemused expression on his face. "Go on."

I ticked the additional suspects off on my fingers. "There's also Star Swift and her plagiarism lawsuit. She showed up to the theater and was shouting accusations. Oh, and crazy knife-wielding fan and her boyfriend."

Detective Keeler got to his feet, taking a scone with him, and wrote on a white board with Holt's ghost floating off to the side. "So Amy Shep's motive would be anger over the book plot, kind of like that character in the *Misery* movie."

"Yes, although Eva told me that although Luanne received a lot of hate mail and the cow's heart before, none of that had ever progressed into an actual attack on her person. But that woman from the brunch… I got the guest list from Nancy just in case someone else was equally upset but waited until later at night to show their displeasure. But the one who returned and got into a fight with Luanne was this Amy Shep."

"She came back later, you said?" The detective turned toward me. "Nothing happened during the brunch itself?"

"No. Everyone was happily chatting about the books, speculating on whether Luanne was going to resurrect him or something. I mean, it is a series about vampires and ghouls, so that's not necessarily out of the question," I added at Keeler's skeptical look. "Luanne shouted that he was dead and was going to stay dead, and things were just kind of subdued and awkward after that. I really don't know why that one woman came back afterward."

The detective made some notes on the board. "I'll check her out. Any of the other guests seem particularly upset? Were there crowds outside the theater holding signs demanding that this character be brought back from the dead? Petitions?"

I got the feeling he was making fun of all this, murder aside. "Well, no, although there probably were when the book was released. It's been a year since Barton Wells was killed off in book six."

"Kind of late in the game to take action, don't you think?" Keeler took another bite of the scone and eyed the board.

"Maybe not." I pulled the list of attendees out of my purse. "Like I said, the topic came up at the brunch, and Luanne flipped her lid. She started screaming that Barton was dead forever and he wasn't going to come back. If a fan was holding on, thinking that Luanne was going to resurrect the character, this might have been the snapping point."

The detective took the list and stuck it on the white board with a magnet. "Suspect two?"

"Knife-wielding woman was in custody during the time of the murder, but she did say there was a Roman protecting the building from ghouls. Maybe Roman got angry that his girlfriend got arrested and decided Luanne was the enemy?" I squirmed a little in my chair. "And I saw him. At least I think it was him. After I called the police and was waiting by the body, this guy wearing a cape came around the cars."

The scone froze halfway to his mouth. "You saw a guy in a cape, and didn't mention it?"

"Why would I mention it?" I asked defensively. "Everyone thought Luanne tripped on those stupid shoes she was wearing and died by accident. Knife-girl was in custody. Even if this was her boyfriend, he seemed absolutely shocked when he saw what I was standing next to. There's no way he's that good of an actor."

The detective scowled. "Even so, I'm questioning him. I'll get his name—his real name— from the girlfriend and bring him in."

"Are there security cameras in the garage?" I asked, suddenly remembering that a city parking deck should have some sort of cameras installed.

He nodded. "Yeah, but from past experience, the surveillance footage from that parking garage is crap. They're mostly focused on the payment machines and where the cars exit. The one near the stairwell might have caught something, if it's not blurry as all heck." He turned back to the white board. "Suspect three?"

"Suspect three would be Star Swift," I told him. "Her plagiarism lawsuit was dismissed, and she was angry enough to come all the way to Milford and publicly confront Luanne in front of everybody in the theater. It was so disruptive that Nancy was thinking of hiring some -off-duty cop as a bouncer for the next speaker."

Keeler put a dot beside the woman's name. "I'm thinking

this case is going to be less about eliminating the suspect pool and more about following the evidence and leads to the killer."

Because there were too many suspects. Even though we had only three on the board, there could be more fans who were furious enough about Barton Wells to kill, or ones who Luanne had been rude to, or ones who felt she'd stolen their ideas. The announcement of a film deal could have been a trigger to anyone harboring a grudge.

Which reminded me.

"There's something going on with the producer guy, Sebastian Codswim. He was angry and very unhappy at the theater—not at all what I'd expect from a guy whose studio had just bought the rights to what is going to be a blockbuster. Eva said it was a legal/contract matter. What if the publisher decided at the last minute to go with a different studio? Or stiffed the company on the rights or something?" I remembered Gerry and her contract. "What if the deal fell through because of something Luanne did or didn't do, and the guy was going to lose his job over it?"

Keeler wrote down the assistant producer's name and a few notes. "Anyone else? This Eva woman might have had enough of Luanne's abuse. Or maybe the innkeeper lady had taken one insult about her cooking too many."

"Maybe." I couldn't see Paula or Gene sneaking up behind Luanne in a parking garage and doing her in. Or Eva. She'd be killing the cash cow. Although, if she'd found out about Gerry, then maybe the knowledge that there was another cash cow might have loosened her inhibitions.

"I don't get why Luanne was in the parking garage at all," I told the detective. "She didn't smoke that I knew of. Why would she have left the theater, gone through that little alleyway and into the parking garage, and walked all the way down to the back exit—all while wearing those absurdly high heels?"

Keeler shrugged. "Maybe she was taking a shortcut to the Mexican place? Or had a phone call she didn't want anyone from the theater to hear? Or maybe she was meeting someone there."

They were all good theories—well, all except for the Mexican place one. Was she placing a desperate call to Gerry about the new contract and hadn't wanted anyone to know? Had someone lured her into the garage by telling her Gerry was there with the contract, only to whack her on the back of the head with...something?

The detective capped the marker and surveyed the board. "I'm still not sure on the murder weapon, though. It was something heavy enough to act as a bludgeon. It broke the skin but didn't leave a huge wound. The M.E. found a tiny sliver of glass in her scalp, so it wasn't a tire iron or a rock."

Glass? "Like someone hit her with a bottle? A beer bottle?"

"Clear glass." Detective Keeler sat back down at his chair and after a moment's hesitation, took another scone. "Thank you for your help, Ms. Carrera. We'll be in touch if we need anything further."

CHAPTER 19

I'd just been dismissed from the police station—and the case—and I wasn't too happy about it. I'd tried J.T.'s line about us being consultants, then I'd bandied Miles' name around, but Detective Keeler hadn't changed his mind. He'd gotten what he wanted from me, including half a dozen of my scones, then waved me out the door.

Jerk. I was tempted to not share any further information with him out of spite, but we both wanted the same thing—to find Luanne's killer and bring him to justice. And only one of us was authorized to make an arrest. Even Holt had deserted me. It should have made me happy that the ghost had stayed behind to haunt the detective, probably rolling pencils and paperclip holders off his desk, but it didn't. His abandonment of me made me feel as if he doubted my abilities to solve this case.

J.T. wasn't expecting me back at the office for a while, so I decided that while I was in Milford, I'd swing by Paula and Gene's and see whether Eva was there or not. She'd not returned my messages, and I was eager to get her the contract copies so she could organize things at the publishing end following Luanne's death. If she wasn't there, maybe I could e-mail them to Gene and have him print them out for me at the inn. That was probably a breach of confidentiality, but oh well.

Imagine my surprise when I walked through the door of the inn and saw Eva there in the living room, papers spread out across the coffee table. There was a manila envelope that looked a lot like the one the manuscript had been in beside her. She looked up at me in surprise, quickly flipping the stacks of papers over.

"Kay! Hi! I'm sorry I haven't called you back. I'm a bit busy with…stuff."

"Well, you're about to be busier. What's your cell phone number?" I plopped down across from her and pulled out my phone, studiously avoiding any glance toward the stacks of papers.

She eyed me suspiciously. "Why? If you've written a book you want to query to me, I have to let you know that it's a really bad time right now. Maybe in a few months—"

"I saw Gerry Pook yesterday." That shut her up. "Luanne had asked me to do a quick detour to see her before her flight, so she was expecting to see her. I've got pics of the contracts—the original one she signed with Luanne and the one she'd gotten a few weeks ago. She hasn't had the new one notarized but was planning on doing it today and mailing them up to you."

Eva let out a whoosh of air and slumped back on the sofa. "Thank goodness! I was pretty sure that was going to be the most awkward conversation ever. She's willing to continue writing the series? And will sign away the film rights? I've been working all morning on getting the publishing company to chip in for a signing bonus to sweeten the deal. We can't lose this film contract. There's too much riding on it."

I wasn't about to tell her Gerry wasn't expecting any further compensation. "I'm sure she'd welcome a bonus, especially since she's been working for a pittance as you'll see when you look at the contract."

That got her moving. I texted her the pictures, verified that she'd received them, then deleted them from my cell phone.

Eva opened up the message, scrolled through the picture, and grimaced. "Yikes. I'll have the publisher draft a new contract with some better terms, although we'll still probably have to pay something to Luanne's estate to license the series titles and to continue using her name on the books. I've got no idea how shark-like her brother is, but we won't want to chance a further lawsuit by screwing him over."

"Is he here yet?" I asked. "Did he fly in this morning to make arrangements?"

She shook her head. "He can't get out until Wednesday, so he asked a local funeral home to take care of...things."

Obviously, she hadn't gotten word yet that Luanne's death wasn't an accident and that the M.E. would probably be keeping the body for a bit longer. No doubt she'd find out soon enough when Detective Keeler showed up to ask her further questions. Until then, I figured I might as well ask some questions of my own.

"Gene told me about that woman coming back. The one with the cow's heart in a box? Amy Shep?"

Eva made an exasperated noise. "Luanne was darned lucky that wasn't the woman with the knife. By the time I got downstairs the pair of them were rolling around the floor, screaming at each other, and yanking hair. I owe the innkeeper for some vase and a little cat statue they smashed."

"I'm surprised you didn't call the police on her," I commented.

"If I called the police every time Luanne pissed someone

off, half of her fans would be in jail. I did what I always do—I smoothed things over. Promised the woman an advance copy, then sent Luanne upstairs where she couldn't insult or attack anyone else."

"I didn't see her at the event. Amy Shep, I mean. Was she there? I figured she would have had a ticket."

Eva shrugged. "Maybe. There were three hundred people there, and I didn't notice her. If she came, she didn't make another scene, and I don't remember seeing her at the meet-and-greet."

"I didn't see that Star woman there either."

The agent's lips tightened into a thin line. "Now I was ready to call the police on her. She knows better than to stick around, though. She said her piece, then probably got on the next plane back to Boston."

"Between those two and the woman with the knife, it was an eventful night," I said as casually as possible.

"Yeah. And then Luanne ends up dead in the parking garage. Those stupid shoes of hers. I always told her she was going to break her neck one day with those." Eva met my eyes. "I'm sorry you had to find her, Kay. I'm sorry anyone had to see her like that. It must have been horrible. Why were you even in the parking garage?"

"I was looking for Luanne. Nancy wanted to have her pose for pictures with some of the guests."

"But the parking garage?" she pressed.

I could hardly tell her a ghost led me to Luanne's body. "I figured maybe she went out for a smoke or decided to grab a taco from the place behind the garage."

"A taco?" Eva laughed. "I would have totally snuck out for a taco, but not Luanne. Not unless the taco was filled with organic bean sprouts and wild-caught Alaskan salmon with gluten-free corn tortillas."

"Why do you think she was in the parking garage?" I

finally got to the question I wanted to ask. "You knew her better than anyone. Why would she have walked out the fire door of the theater, through the alleyway and the entire length of the parking garage in those crazy shoes?"

Eva looked down at the stacks of papers. "Perhaps she had a private phone call she needed to make."

Gerry hadn't mentioned hearing from Luanne that night. In fact, she'd told me she hadn't heard from Luanne after Friday night. Was there anyone else who Luanne would have needed to have a private phone conversation with? Because I doubted there was anyone in Milford she would have been meeting in the back of the parking garage.

"Well, the police have her phone now. They'll figure it out if she was calling someone or not." I stood.

"What? Why would the police have her phone? Why would they be checking to see if she was calling someone or not when she fell?" Eva had jumped to her feet as well, twisting her hands together in front of her.

"I meant they'd have the phone because it was on her body when they took it away. And last thing I knew, there was no law against distracted walking, so I doubt they'd have any reason to check her calls." I shrugged. "Her brother probably will though."

Eva sat back down. "Yeah. Maybe. Well, thanks for stopping by. I really appreciate you taking it upon yourself to go see Gerry and get those contracts." She looked at me once more, her gaze sharp as it met mine. "Why did you do that? How did you know who she was and her address? From what I can see, Luanne kept that very much a secret."

I smiled at her then turned to leave. "Oh, I work for a private investigative firm, so there's not much I can't figure out. Good luck, Eva. Hope things work out with the film deal."

CHAPTER 20

When I walked into my office, there was a young man sitting at a chair by J.T.'s desk. My boss glanced over at me with raised eyebrows, then inclined his head.

I shot him a puzzled glance, then the young man turned and I stopped dead in my tracks.

"He said he was going to wait for you," J.T. told me, then turned to the boy. "She's here. Say what you need to say."

Boy, because every man younger than thirty seemed a boy to me, and this young man in particular. I knew him. Even without the cape I knew him.

"You recognize me?" he asked, getting to his feet. "Lanie just texted me and said the police are looking for me. I didn't have anything to do with that woman's death. You saw me. You saw me there in the parking garage. You know I didn't kill her."

He'd taken a step toward me and J.T., bless his heart, angled himself between the two of us. "You just keep your distance, boy. Understand me?"

It seemed I wasn't the only one who thought every man younger than thirty was a boy.

"I take it Lanie is the woman who was arrested at the theater? The one with the knife?" I edged closer to my desk where I had a very heavy stapler, just in case. "And you were the Roman wannabe from the parking garage. I did see you there, but I didn't see who killed Luanne. For all I know, you murdered her, then circled back around to make yourself look like you were completely innocent."

'Roman's eyes grew wide. "I *am* innocent. It was just a cosplay. Lanie's really into the novels and likes to act them out. We didn't mean to hurt anyone. I was supposed to patrol the area for ghouls, but after an hour of walking around the garage, I went to a pub. When Lanie didn't text me, I went back to the garage to look for her. That's when I saw you. I got scared that maybe Lanie had gotten carried away and took off. She called me on Sunday when she made bail and I picked her up. She didn't even know the woman was dead. I didn't do anything. It's not against the law to walk around a building or parking garage. Not like I was trespassing or anything."

"You're going to need to talk to the police," I told him. "I mentioned to the detective that I'd seen you in the garage, and that you seemed quite shocked to see the body, but you'll need to give him the details of where you were. Hopefully someone at that pub can verify you were there at the time of death."

"When *were* you at the garage?" J.T. asked him. "Did you hear anything before you gave up hunting for ghouls and headed for the pub?"

The guy frowned. "I probably walked around for an hour or so. A few cars left. I heard some people talking and walking around. Car doors and the sound of them starting.

Oh, and that stupid machine that yells to pay before leaving every time someone comes within two feet of it."

"Anyone on that level? Arguing? The sound of someone getting hit with something?" I asked.

He shook his head slowly. "Things echo in that garage. I heard two women, but I'm not sure if they were talking loudly or what. Then there was that couple smooching by their car—I think they might have come from the Mexican place. And the sound of car doors closing...that might have been someone getting hit. I'm not really sure."

Well, that was really not much help at all.

"Are they going to arrest me?" The boy looked back and forth between me and J.T.

"Probably not, but if they do, I know a good bail bond company." My boss grinned and handed the guy a card before escorting him out the door.

"I wasn't sure about that guy," J.T. confessed when he came back in. "No way was I going to leave you alone with him. He was nervous as all heck, sweating and fidgeting around in his chair."

"Well, he's a lot less scary without the cape," I told him. "I don't think he did it. I saw the look on his face when he came around the corner in that parking garage and found Luanne sprawled across the floor."

"So who *did* do it?" J.T. eyed the few remaining scones in my container. "Did you manage to sweeten that detective up with those things?"

I snorted. "Not enough. I got some information out of him, but he got more out of me. And I'm pretty sure he's not interested in using us as consultants. I got the 'we'll call you if we have any more questions' spiel."

"So, what did you find out?" J.T. pulled out his chair and plopped down.

"That Luanne was hit on the back of the head with something hard enough that she fell forward onto the step and broke her neck. That whatever was used to hit her had some sort of glass in it because there were a few small shards in her hair and scalp."

"A bottle?" J.T. mused.

"That's what I thought but it would need to be a clear bottle. And if it shattered enough to leave small shards behind, where was the rest of the glass? I didn't see anything on the ground around Luanne, and if someone threw a bottle at her or whacked her on the head with one, there should have been chunks of broken glass."

"Maybe he picked them up?"

I scowled. "Big pieces, yes, but do you really think a murderer would hang around long enough to clean up every tiny little bit of broken glass?"

"You're right. And shards small enough that the first responders didn't notice would make me think of a thinner glass than a bottle." J.T. looked around his desk. "How about a cell phone?"

I looked down at mine. "Aren't they shatterproof? I mean, I've seen the screens crack, but not enough to have glass fall out of them."

"Not all of them are shatterproof, and I absolutely have seen one break to the point that little bits of glass fell out of it. If they didn't have a screen protector and had one heck of a pitching arm, they could have hit her hard enough to leave glass behind."

"Or what if the screen was already cracked? It might not even take a heck of a pitching arm to leave glass behind in that instance. And with Luanne's crazy shoes, it wouldn't take much to knock her forward onto the ground."

"Then the killer scoops his broken phone up off the ground and runs off," J.T. concluded. "In and out in no time. And they'd probably still have the murder weapon, because they'd want to transfer all their pictures and contacts and everything to a new one."

"Not necessarily," I told him. "Most people have their phone contents backed up on a cloud service. The killer could easily throw it away, get a new one, and be back in business with a few minutes of download."

"There would still be a record of that," J.T. countered. "Once the police have a suspect, they can check to see if the guy loaded his stuff onto a new phone sometime after Saturday night."

"The problem is the police don't have a suspect." I rolled my eyes. "Actually, they probably have too many suspects. Even if we rule out that Roman impersonator, there's still tons of people who had motive, and just as many who had opportunity. Detective Keeler is going to try to find the murder weapon and try to track the killer that way."

"Is he going to pull surveillance from the garage?"

I nodded. "But he doesn't think he'll find much. Most of the cameras are on the pay machines, the stairwells, and the place where the cars exit. There's a camera in the general area where I found Luanne, but Keeler thinks it's probably not pointed the right way and would be such poor quality that he might not be able to get anything from it."

J.T. narrowed his eyes. "He might want to check with Manny."

"Who the heck is Manny?" Did I mention J.T. knew pretty much everyone in the county? Another reason he and Daisy would be a good fit, in my opinion.

"Emmanuel Clarke. He owns the Mexican place that backs up to the parking garage. A few years back he had some problems with his dumpster being set on fire and put in a few security cameras. And unlike the city of Milford, Manny actually sprung for some fairly expensive ones. Didn't want his building catching on fire because some idiot liked to throw lit cigarettes or whatever in his dumpster."

My heartbeat picked up at the thought that we might have a lead that Detective Keeler didn't. I eyed my phone, thinking of how smug I'd feel calling him with the tip.

"Go talk to Manny first." It was as if J.T. had read my mind. "Tell him I sent you. Check out if there's anything on his tapes, then walk into the Milford PD, plop them down on Detective Keeler's desk, and give him the finger."

I laughed. "Giving him the finger probably isn't going to make Detective Keeler or anyone else at Milford PD ever want to use us as consultants."

He grinned. "Okay, so don't give him the finger. But *do* let him know that we're available for low, low rates."

I knew J.T. and his rates were far from low, but he was right. It would be awesome to put another notch in our investigative successes belt—well, in *my* investigative successes belt. I'd already provided a lot of valuable information, but to walk up to the detective with a tape that clearly showed the crime…

"So, I'm okay to take the rest of the day off?" I asked J.T.

He waved his hand at me. "This is business, Kay. We might not have a paying client on this one, but it's publicity and that's business. Go. Say 'hi' to Manny for me. And make sure to get a pork tamale while you're there."

CHAPTER 21

I parked in the garage, fairly close to where I'd found Luanne, and walked around a bit, examining it all with fresh eyes. It was about half full—no doubt a mixture of people who worked in the downtown area and those enjoying a nice summer day walking among the shops and parks in the area. Heading out into the narrow alleyway, I decided to retrace my steps from Saturday night before heading over to the Mexican place.

The theater's fire door was shut tight, the alley dirty with grime and soot but in spite of a few cigarette butts, surprisingly clean. Heading through the open doorway to the garage, I climbed the few stairs, tried not to jump as the machine sternly told me to pay before returning to my car, then headed toward the rear exit. My footsteps sounded abnormally loud in the echo of the building. Sound seemed to be so amplified here that if the Roman impersonator had been in the parking deck at the time of Luanne's murder, I felt sure he would have heard something—the voices, the scuffle, a scream or a cry as she fell, the rushed footsteps of the murderer running away.

I stood in front of the rear door and stared at the three steps, envisioning the scene from two nights ago. Luanne's ghost was there—a faint shadow that flitted from the stairwell to the doorway then back again. She didn't seem to notice me, and again I got the feeling her spirit wasn't long for this world. The area was squeaky clean compared to the rest of the parking garage, but I could still see in my mind Luanne's form sprawled at the bottom of the step along with the misty gray of her ghost.

"She would have been standing here," I mused out loud as I took the position. "Facing this way. So whoever hit her would have been here. Unless he or she threw something at her."

They would have had to be fairly close though because with the parked cars and the way the vestibule was put together, an attacker farther than a few feet wouldn't have had a clear shot at Luanne. I hadn't even seen her until I'd come around that last line of cars. Was Luanne here talking with someone? Or was she on her phone, facing so she was looking out of the parking garage into the lights of the small road and the back of the businesses? There was nothing here to tell me whether she was attacked by someone she knew, or while she was distracted on the phone.

Or whether she was trying to flee. Maybe someone had hit her over the head and she was running away in those crazy shoes and tripped. Maybe that's why there hadn't been any other glass at the scene.

But there hadn't been glass or blood in the path I'd taken to get here from the theater, and my gut told me that Luanne hadn't run all over the parking deck in those shoes. Even from the theater to here was a stretch for someone who loudly proclaimed she couldn't walk three blocks in her footwear of choice.

Sighing in frustration, I climbed the three steps and out into the daylight of the little road that ran behind the theater and other businesses. It was a named road, but in reality, little more than a wide alleyway. There were parking spots marked here and there, no doubt for the people who owned the different businesses and came in and out through their back entrances. Six dumpsters lined the road, tucked neatly against the buildings. Each door had a light above it, ensuring some safety for the folks who worked here and might need to enter and exit through these doors at night. Hopefully that meant the video from the Mexican place would be reasonably clear.

Sure enough, a shiny black camera was mounted high beside one doorway, pointed to cover the steps and the dumpster. I went to stand near it and realized that while it might have caught some footage of the doorway to the parking garage, it wasn't angled to get a good view of what was happening right inside. But I was standing on the ground and the camera was a good ten to twelve feet up, so it was worth a look.

Walking down the roadway, I headed around to the front of the businesses. The faint sounds of Mariachi music grew louder as I neared Taco Bonanza. Inside, the atmosphere was festive with a sea of colorful chairs and tables, rows of sombreros on shelves near the ceiling, and a huge mural of a couple performing the tango in front of Mayan ruins along the rear wall. When I asked for Manny, the blonde girl at the bar stuck her head through the back doorway and shouted for him.

A tall, dark-haired, middle-aged man came toward me. I couldn't take my eyes off his mustachios, waxed into little curls at the end as if he were a villain about to tie me across a set of train tracks.

"Manny Clarke." He stuck out his hand and I shook it,

half expecting him to twirl the ends of the mustache with his other hand.

"Kay Carrera." I dug a business card out of my bag and handed it to him. "My boss is J.T. Pierson. He asked me to stop by and see if I could look at your surveillance footage from Saturday night. There was a woman—"

His eyes widened, and he pocketed my card without even looking at it. "The woman who died? Saints above, is that a crime now? She didn't fall?"

I bit my tongue, not wanting to let something out that wasn't public knowledge yet. "She was a well-known author, and I was helping with the event. We just wanted to see if your camera caught what happened when she fell."

"Ah." He nodded. "Insurance liability and all that. I get it. I swear it seems like every time someone slips and falls, they get a million-dollar settlement. Sorry this woman died and all that but sliding on a banana peel doesn't mean the city should pay a bunch of money to her estate."

I shrugged, trying to look as if I were no more in the know that he was. "It's probably nothing. J.T. just asked me to swing by and see if you could show me the footage."

He waved for me to follow him. I turned to quickly ask the bartender to put in couple of tamale orders to go for me, then went after Manny, through the kitchen and into a tiny back room that doubled as dry-goods storage and an office.

The chair squawked as he sat. He clicked on a graphic and pulled up a program, fast forwarding through a set of black and white images. "When did it happen?"

"Between nine and nine-thirty, give or take a few minutes."

He halted the footage, backed it up a bit, then set it to play at triple speed. "Let me know if you want me to pause anywhere and slow it down."

There was no sound, and for the first ten minutes of the

tape, the only action was an employee from a neighboring business having a smoke, and one of Manny's employees coming out to toss a trash bag into the dumpster. Finally, at nine-twenty, I could see what looked like someone near the parking garage doorway. I had Manny back it up and play it several times, even slowing it down to frame-by-frame, but from the way the camera was positioned, I could only see vague movement and a shape pitching forward.

I sat back and sighed, rubbing my forehead. So much for this idea. Hopefully Detective Keeler would have better luck with the cameras in the garage. Just when I was about to thank Manny for his time, collect my tamales, and go, I saw a figure exit the doorway into the street behind the restaurant.

"Wait. Pause it." I leaned closer to the screen but couldn't make out who the person was. She was female, tall, with hair that looked dark in the black-and-white video. I advanced it slowly, watching the woman walk toward the dumpster, look up and down the roadway, then lift the lid a bit to slide something in. With another quick glance, she turned and instead of going back into the parking deck, she slipped down the narrow alleyway between the deck and the theater.

The video was grainy, but I recognized her. Then I looked at the time. Nine twenty-five. I'd headed out to look for Luanne at just before nine thirty. She'd walked down the alleyway and slipped inside the propped-open fire door to the theater just as I'd started to go look for Luanne. Had she been the killer? Or had someone come up and murdered Luanne in the five minutes between her leaving the parking garage and my entering it?

And more importantly, what the heck had she stuck in the dumpster?

"When do you guys have garbage pickup?"

"Tomorrow morning," Manny told me.

"Do you mind if I go check in your dumpster?"

He laughed. "Knock yourself out. It's gonna be kinda smelly after the weekend, what with the heat we've had this month. I'll have Sheila hold your tamales up at the bar for when you're done."

"Thanks." I stood up. "Can you make a copy of the footage?" I wanted to run it by the police station, and maybe give Detective Keeler the finger as I put it on his desk.

"Sure. Tell J.T. he owes me one."

I left my purse with him for safekeeping and headed out the back door, wrinkling my nose as I saw—and smelled—the dumpster. I'd seen it earlier when I left the parking garage, but up close, it was quite fragrant. And when I flipped the lid up, the smell nearly gagged me.

Hopping up on the lip of the trash container, I peered inside and saw only black garbage bags. Ugh. This was going to be disgusting, but whatever the woman in the image had put in here, it had obviously slid down between these bags. I lifted them out one at a time until there was a smelly line of black beside the container. Then I leaned forward, grimacing as I tried in vain to reach the other bags.

I'd have to climb in. And then I'd need to burn my clothes and spend a few hours scrubbing myself raw in a hot shower to get rid of this smell. I pulled myself up and over the edge of the dumpster, silently thanking Daisy for all those early-morning yoga sessions that meant I was still fit enough to do this sort of thing. Then I dropped as carefully as I could feet-first into the container, wincing as I felt something squish under my shoes.

Trying to hold my breath, I sorted through the bags, tossing a few more over the edge into the road and hoping that they didn't break open. Just as I was about ready to give up and just leave the whole stinky mess to Detective Keeler, my foot hit something hard. I bent down and groped around under a few smaller bags, my hand closing on something that felt like a hard, thin rectangle.

It was a tablet. I pulled it up and saw the cracked screen, the smear of red across the surface. Blood? Or salsa from one of the broken bags? It was hard to tell, but one thing was sure —I really shouldn't have been handling this thing without gloves on because I was confident that I'd just discovered the murder weapon.

I eyed it with smug satisfaction. This plus Manny's video would be all the proof the police would need. Even if the red smudge was hot sauce, I was sure they could match the glass from Luanne's head wound to this broken screen. And a quick run through their IT folks would show exactly who it was registered to.

"I believe that's mine."

I looked up to see a knife in my face. It was the sort of stabby thing used to fillet fish and the hand it was attached to belonged to Eva Zinovi. I backed up a few steps, nearly tripping on a garbage bag. The dumpster made it impossible for me to run away, but its height and positioning against the building made it also difficult for Eva to reach across the lip and stab me without falling in herself.

"Hand it over." She held out the hand that wasn't holding the knife.

"It's the murder weapon." It was probably a dumb thing to say, but at this point I was pretty sure that she knew I knew.

Something flickered in her dark eyes. Desperation. I eyed the knife, realizing that she was probably thinking the same thing I was—she could take the tablet and dispose of it, but I *knew*. And the only chance she'd have of getting away with this was if I were dead.

"It's not a murder weapon." Her voice was cool as she leaned forward, reaching for the tablet. "I didn't mean for her to die. I just.... I'd just had it with her. Years I'd put up with her demands and nasty attitude, years I got her the best deals, negotiated the best contracts, and here she was a talentless hack. Actually, she was a talentless hack that almost lost us a multimillion dollar film deal."

"You made out pretty good over the years," I told her, holding the tablet just out of her reach. "And it was a simple fix. Luanne had already sent a new contract to Gerry. By the end of this week you would have had a contract to show the publisher and the studio that full rights had been waived to Luanne. Everything would have worked out okay."

"No, it wouldn't have been okay," she snapped. "Do you know how humiliating it is to have some producer tell you that your client had a ghostwriter, and that the studio needed to have a copy of that contract in order to close the deal? A ghostwriter. And guess who looks like either a deceiving liar or an idiot in front of both the publishing house and the studio? Not Luanne. Me. I'm the one who was representing her. I'm the one left holding the bag at the end of the day. I'm the one who they'd never do business with again. Luanne would have gotten a slap on the wrist. Maybe she would have been pushed out of future contracts and the publishing house would have gone direct to the ghostwriter or negotiated a lesser deal for Luanne, but me? My career was *over*. And it was all her fault."

"And it's not now?" I pressed. "Luanne is dead, and there's still the ghostwriter issue that's come to light."

"But now I'm the hero," she countered. "Bumbling, lying, stupid Luanne dies because of her choice in footwear, and I jump in to button up the ghostwriter contract and save the day. I get my cut of everything. The film deal goes forward. And I never have to deal with that lying piece of work ever again. Now, hand me the tablet."

She wouldn't get away with it. Detective Keeler would see the video tape, bring her in for questioning, and some evidence somewhere would implicate her, even if it wasn't this tablet. Still, I didn't want to just give it over, and I wanted to make sure I lived to see the morning, so I made her reach as far as she could into the dumpster before handing her the tablet.

I kept a hold of my side, yanking as she tried to pull it back, and swinging a garbage bag toward her. She stabbed with the knife, gutting the garbage bag, and I shoved forward, pushing the bag aside and to the grimy floor of the dumpster, taking the knife with it. Unfortunately, the very action I took to disarm Eva allowed her to regain her balance and stay on the outside of the container. She shrieked in frustration and jerked the tablet from my hand, swinging it toward my head. I raised my hand and ducked, taking the impact of the tablet on my arm. My foot slipped on the slimy floor of the dumpster and I fell to the side, banging my shoulder on the metal. Before I could scramble to my feet, the lid of the dumpster slammed shut and I was plunged into smelly darkness.

My first thought was one of relief. Her knife was stuck in a garbage bag somewhere in this dumpster. Yes, she had the tablet, but closing the plastic lid on the container wouldn't hold me for long. I'd just wait for a few minutes for her to leave, then lift the lid and climb out and call the cops. The lid was heavy, but it was plastic for crying out loud. I'd manage.

Then I began to hear the thumps of stuff being piled on top of the dumpster and I panicked. Standing, I shoved at the lid in vain, feeling the oppressive August heat beginning to amplify in the closed metal container, and nearly choking on the sickening smell of garbage.

Worse, I didn't have my purse, which meant I didn't have my phone to call for help. All I could do was bang on the lid and kick at the metal sides of the dumpster and hope that someone would hear me and come to the rescue. It had to be close to five. People would be getting off work and maybe coming down this little road to get to the parking garage. Hopefully Manny's staff would soon come out with another garbage bag to toss in and release me.

Hopefully one of those things would happen soon because I was quickly becoming drenched in sweat. How long before I succumbed to heat stroke? The sun would be dipping low enough that the dumpster wouldn't be in direct light soon and would hopefully cool off. Eventually someone would come out to dump trash. Worst case scenario was I'd be found tomorrow morning when the trash collection people came. I winced, thinking about one of those giant trash trucks' mechanical arms tipping the dumpster upright and into the truck while I screamed for help, and decided that spending the night in the smelly hot container wasn't the worst part of that scenario.

A shadow formed in the corner of the dumpster and I shivered, grateful this time for the chill a ghost brought. And the company was nice, even if he couldn't talk to me or do anything besides roll potatoes off counters.

Wait. Poltergeist.

"Holt! Can you open the dumpster lid? I'm stuck in here."

The lid thumped a few times. I heard something roll off the top and stood, trying to add my strength to that of the ghost. Sadly, the lid didn't budge more than a fraction of an inch. I sat on a garbage bag and huffed in exasperation. It wasn't Holt's fault. He was a ghost. I couldn't open the lid and I was in a solid corporeal form. I guess the limit to his abilities were potatoes and wine glasses. After a few seconds, even the ghost abandoned me.

I waited, listening for anyone coming by and trying to conserve my energy and not breathe in any more of the garbage fumes than I had to. The light dimmed, filtering through the cracks where the lid had warped and didn't fit tightly against the metal of the container, telling me that it was getting on toward evening. Five o'clock? Six? How long had I been stuck in here?

I was thinking about searching for the fillet knife while I still had a tiny bit of light, just in case I needed to defend myself, when I heard the rustling sound of something being scraped across the lid of the container.

"Hey! I'm trapped in here! Let me out!" I placed a few sharp kicks to the side of the dumpster and heard a high-pitched shriek, then the thump of something hitting the ground. The dumpster lid flew open, and I looked up to see the blonde bartender from Manny's—Sheila.

"You scared me half to death," she scolded. "What are you doing in there? You never came back in for your tamales. Plus, I was more than a bit irritated that you left all the trash bags piled on top of the lid instead of throwing them back in."

I scrambled up the side of the container, throwing my leg over and gratefully taking Sheila's offered hand.

"Normally I wouldn't have come out here," she continued, "but an entire tray of dishes tipped over on the stand. It was a horrible mess—enchiladas and refried beans everywhere. No sooner did I get that cleaned up then the same thing happened to another tray. I filled two garbage bags and wanted to get them out before the dinner rush started. It was really weird. Paco in the kitchen said all his potatoes kept rolling off the counters, too. Weird stuff. Like we were haunted or something."

Holt. I owed him a big thank you the next time he appeared. A really big thank you.

"Someone locked me in and took the evidence I was looking for," I told Sheila. "I'm glad you came out when you did, or I would have probably been stuck in there until you guys closed. I need to get my purse from Manny's office and call the police."

Sheila wrinkled her nose. "No offense, but you stink. Stay here and I'll bring the purse out to you. And your tamales."

She vanished inside the building only to come back a few minutes later holding my purse, a bag, and a USB stick. "Manny says the tamales are on the house, and here's the footage copy you wanted from the surveillance cam." I went to dig in my purse for a tip and she waved me away. "Catch me next time."

"Thanks," I called back to her as I ran for the parking garage. No doubt she didn't want my stinky hands all over her tip. Honestly, I didn't want my stinky hands inside my purse, fumbling with my phone, or my stinky self plopped down on my car's upholstery as I simultaneously tried to dial the police and swipe my credit card in the exit to the garage.

I tore down the city streets, on hold for Detective Keeler and violating the hands-free cell phone laws. Milford isn't all that big a city, and the police department had me on hold forever, so I'd actually parked and was through the metal detector before he picked up.

"It's Eva Zinovi," I blurted out breathlessly as I took the stairs to the police department entrance and yet another security check. "Manny had her on video tape exiting the parking garage right around the time Luanne was killed and then she threw something in the trash bin. I went dumpster diving and found the broken tablet, but she showed up with a knife and took it and locked me in the dumpster."

"What? Who? You're inside a dumpster?"

"No, I'm here in the station, waiting to go through the second scanner. The bartender let me out of the dumpster. I've got a copy of the footage, but you need to get Eva. Put out an APB or lock down the airport or something because she's going to get away."

The huge metal door on the other side of the security area opened and Detective Keeler stood there, cell phone to his ear. We stared at each other a minute, then he hung up and walked around the scanner.

I held out the USB stick and he stared at it, wrinkling his nose.

"Carrera, you stink."

"Well, I *have* been trapped in a garbage container for…" I looked at my phone. "Thirty minutes."

Thirty minutes? It sure as heck seemed longer than that.

"Come on." He waved me through the scanner and took me back to his workspace and immediately began opening desk drawers.

"Aren't you going to call the state police?" I insisted. "Homeland Security or whoever is in charge of the airport? Do you think she'll try to fly back to New York, or head for Mexico?"

He pulled a can out of the bottom drawer of his desk. "Shut your eyes."

I did what he said and heard the hiss of the spray can. The overpowering scent of gardenias filled my nose.

"There. That's better. Whatever you do, don't sit in any of the chairs. I don't even think this stuff will get the smell out."

"Here." I thrust the USB stick at him once more. "You need to catch her before she flees the country. I'm sure she's already ditched that tablet again."

Detective Keeler took the stick gently and plugged it into his computer. We both watched the grainy photo of the woman exiting the parking garage, slipping something into the dumpster, and walking back to the theater down the alleyway.

"See the time?" I pointed to his screen, careful not to touch it. "She came into the theater, and less than five minutes later, I saw her in the bathroom, cleaning up. Then I went out to look for Luanne and found her in the parking garage. Luanne had to have been killed before she walked out of the parking garage. There just wasn't enough time for someone else to do it between her entering the theater and my finding Luanne."

"Mmmm," Detective Keeler mused.

"And she exited the parking garage door where Luanne was laying right in front of the step," I continued. "She had to have hopped over her to get out that door. So, she either killed Luanne, or she callously stepped over a dead body, threw something in a dumpster, went back into the theater, then told me she had no idea where Luanne was. And the broken tablet…I'm sure it was hers. And it had blood on it, or maybe salsa, I'm not sure."

"And she locked you in the dumpster."

"Yes, and threatened me with a knife. She tried to stab me, but I deflected the knife with a garbage bag."

The detective had sounded rather amused, which was irritating the heck out of me. I'd just been locked in a dumpster. A little sympathy would have been appreciated.

"I guess we'll add assault with a deadly weapon to the charges, then." Detective Keeler pulled the USB stick from the computer and put it inside a plastic bag, writing something on the front.

"Are you going to put a warrant out on her?" I insisted, perplexed by his casual slow-as-molasses attitude. "You might want to get on that before she vanishes in the wind. Today might be a good idea."

He leaned back in his chair and steepled his hands, looking at me over the tops of his fingers. "We already have her in custody. While you were rooting around a dumpster, Mrs. Carrera, I was interviewing people and reviewing camera footage from the parking deck. Two witnesses saw Ms. Zinovi go out for a smoke around nine fifteen. Five minutes later, Ms. Trainor asked a witness where Ms. Zinovi was and followed her into the parking deck. Camera footage shows the two walking toward the back of the deck and obviously having a verbal altercation. With the time stamp on that video, we had reasonable suspicion to call Ms. Zinovi in for questioning. We found her hurriedly loading her things into a rental car outside of Billingsly's. And in her possession was a tablet with a broken screen, some glass missing, and with a red substance that was most definitely not salsa on it."

I let out my breath in a whoosh. "You caught her. Did she confess?"

He rocked in his chair, causing it to squawk a bit. "No, she lawyered up. But we've got her."

"She confessed to me," I told him. "I can testify to that as well as her trying to stab me and locking me in the dumpster."

He sat forward and fixed me with a rather intense stare. "I owe you my thanks. We've got a good case, but this additional footage plus your testimony will help."

That meant a lot. "Maybe you'll consider using Pierson Investigative and Recovery Services as a consultant on future cases?"

He grinned. "Don't push your luck, Carrera. Now go home and shower. You stink."

I grinned back and spun on my heel, hardly noticing the ache in my arm and shoulder as I practically skipped out of the station. He'd definitely consider using us in the future. And he was right—I did stink.

CHAPTER 22

J.T. was right—the tamales were amazing. I'd managed to make it home before Judge Beck and was able to shower and even put through my clothes through a heavy-stain cycle in the washer before he came through the door. Then I told him all about my adventures over tamales and a big chef salad. I left out the part about being nearly stabbed and being locked in a dumpster for half an hour. My arm and shoulder were feeling better thanks to some aspirin, and I wanted him to see me more as the savvy almost-detective and not the woman who gets trapped in a dumpster by a murderer. I had a habit of finding murder victims. I didn't need to add the habit of being nearly killed by murderers to that.

After dinner, the judge spread all his papers out on the dining room table and went to work. I was just settling in with the second Fanged Darkness book when a shadow appeared over by the bookcase.

"I was wondering when you'd show up." I whispered the words, not wanting Judge Beck to hear me and think I was in here talking to myself. "Mystery's solved. Murderer is behind bars. Take a hike and I'll see you tomorrow at work. It's going to be boring stuff from here on out, though. That stuff today doesn't happen all the time, so don't think you're going to be rescuing me from dumpsters and helping me find murder victims several times a week."

The spirit darkened and moved closer. His presence felt heavy, insistent.

"Thank you, by the way," I told him. "I'm not sure how long I would have been stuck in that dumpster if you hadn't helped. I really appreciate it."

Holt stayed where he was and I shivered at a sudden blast of cold. The front window frosted over, then cleared, just like Olive's mirror.

The mirror.

I got up and snuck behind Judge Beck as quietly as I could so as to not disturb him. Then I slid open the silverware drawer of the sideboard and took the mirror out. Walking on tiptoes, I headed back into the parlor and set the heavy mirror on the coffee table.

It immediately frosted over, neat block lettering filling the surface.

Can't imagine Sherlock Holmes getting locked in a dumpster.

Ha, ha. Yeah, thanks. I scowled at the mirror.

Or those guys from NCIS. Or Gator Pierson.

"*Gator* would totally get trapped in a dumpster," I hissed. "He'd just make sure he didn't film that part."

The mirror frosted over again. *It was fun, but not as much fun as football.*

I suddenly felt bad for the guy once more. "No, I'm sure it's not as much fun as football."

Season starts soon. I miss it. I miss the guys. I'm thinking I might head to Atlanta and haunt them for a bit.

"Won't that be like rubbing salt in the wound?" I asked the ghost. "How difficult will it be for you to watch them play, knowing it could have been you out there with them? Knowing you'll never be able to do that again?"

The frost on the mirror slowly melted and I wondered for a moment if I'd upset him.

It's going to be hard, but I want to watch them. Maybe help them.

I grimaced at the thought of a poltergeist helping an NFL team. Guess we wouldn't be seeing Atlanta in the Super Bowl this year.

"If it's too painful and you want to come back, you're welcome here." What was I saying? "Well, you're welcome here sometimes. Only when I'm working or at barbeques, and only if you leave Taco's food bowl alone."

Ugh. I hate your cat.

I laughed. "My cat hates you."

I wanted to say goodbye and thank you. You made this easier for me. And I don't think I ever laughed as hard as I did when you got locked in that dumpster.

"Glad I could be of comedic value." I looked up at the shadow, and for once he wasn't just in the corner of my vision but right in front of me. "Good luck, Holt. I'll miss you."

Well, kind of.

Yeah, you'll miss me. You and all the other hot bit—ladies. All the other hot ladies.

I laughed, then watched as the shadow faded and the words vanished from the mirror, leaving the surface clear and wet. I hope wherever the ghost went, he found his peace.

I knew I had. With a contented sigh, I curled up on the couch, picked up my book, and lost myself in a world of vampires and ghouls.

ACKNOWLEDGMENTS

Special thanks to Lyndsey Lewellen for cover design and typography, and to both Erin Zarro and Jennifer Cosham for copyediting.

ABOUT THE AUTHOR

Libby Howard lives in a little house in the woods with her sons and two exuberant bloodhounds. She occasionally knits, occasionally bakes, and occasionally manages to do a load of laundry. Most of her writing is done in a bar where she can combine work with people-watching, a decent micro-brew, and a plate of Old Bay wings.

For more information:
libbyhowardbooks.com/

ALSO BY LIBBY HOWARD

Locust Point Mystery Series:

The Tell All

Junkyard Man

Antique Secrets

Hometown Hero

A Literary Scandal

Root of All Evil (August 2018)

CPSIA information can be obtained
at www.ICGtesting.com
Printed in the USA
BVHW030352240920
589460BV00003B/288

9 781733 069144